Claudine Fisher

CALL ME CAROLE

A Novel

Photo by French photographer Pierre Baudier and cover design by Pat Carew

La vie est un voyageur qui laisse traîner son manteau derrière lui pour effacer ses traces.

Life is a voyager who lets his coat drag behind him to erase his footprints.
Louis Aragon (1942)

1

MOI
Autumn 1971

Let me introduce myself. My name is Carol. I am no devil, I am no angel. No, that's not good enough. Let me start again. *Je m'appelle Carole.* I prefer Carole with an 'e' please, because of my French ancestry. *Bonjour. Je suis Carole*, the newly-born woman.

I was born somewhere, obviously. You are going to ask me 'where?' you smart aleck. You think you are smart, don't you? I'll concede that you're smart, if that makes you feel better. Oh, yes, I've heard it before, we're all born and we're all going to die. It's true, it's trite, so why do we repeat the obvious? It is one thing we all have in common, we silly humans. We die, yet we act as though we'll never die. We forget that chimpanzees' DNA is almost identical to ours. Even I, though I should know better, forget it all the time. *Oh, mon semblable, mon frère,* as Baudelaire would say: you are like me, my brother... and my sister. We're built this way. Very clever way of being built, really, forgetting the essentials. Now, where was I? Well, at birth. Let's begin again.

I wished I was not born in the harsh inland climate of Chicago, Illinois, USA, where you feel the raw cold of winter and sultry heat of summer. Who'd want to be born there? So, I created another identity for myself. I was born in God's country and do you know where that is? In the South of France, naturally. Where else? Where verdant groves produce the best tasting oranges, lemons and tangerines, where the fragrance of lavender hangs in the air mingled with the sweet aroma of overripe figs, where thyme and myrrh grow in your garden two steps from your kitchen window and where you can also pick parsley and basil to toss into the pot.

In Provence, you can make true tomatoes *à la provençale*, with lots of garlic. There, your food tastes as good as it should. Being born in France means that you know the difference between Chanel No.5 and Ivory Soap.

By the way, do you know what the inhabitants of the South of France repeat *ad vitam aeternam*? You know the story, God created the earth in six days. If you ask me, He was not a very fast worker since He could do anything He wanted, and as fast as He wanted. But it took Him six days to create the world. On the morning of the seventh, He decided to rest because He was exhausted, that's how I remember the story. At that juncture, He noticed he had a little dirt left in His hand. Lo and behold, what could He do with it, before He took a nap? God was puzzled. Throw it away! Get rid of it! Any child with dirt in his hand could have told God that, I hear you. And God knew that too...

So, God threw the handful of dirt away. With a beautiful gesture, like the hand of the farmer sowing his seed and his seeds, to the wind, whoosh, to the four winds, to that little forgotten corner of the world, that corner which was the South of France. True heaven on earth.

And I, Carole, that's where I decided that I COME FROM. It used to be heaven on earth at that time, when I was a little girl. Except that after the Impressionists discovered Southern France and painted it, the British discovered it and exposed their pink and white skin to its sun, the White Russians discovered it, and the writers discovered it and wrote about it. Colette, good French girl that she was, coming from Nivernais, Burgundy, in fact, was one of those early guilty writers. Add to that movie stars like Brigitte Bardot and her followers, and thousands of bare-breasted starlets and other amazons in long succession since… and, of course, tourists discovered it and developers and builders. Now the Riviera has become Hell with a twist, in a martini glass!

We were done in, we locals in the South of France. Shame on them all. Saint-Tropez, Cannes, Nice, Monaco, the Riviera, *Côte d'Azur,* all of it was gradually spoilt. The azure sky and the mistral wind remained, but the rest of it has gone down the drain.

That is why I chose yet another corner of the world, Oregon, to settle in with my little family and build a cozy nest in the middle of nowhere, a small house in the woods.

Listen a minute, will you! Don't be so impatient. I'll get there, to the heart of my tale. I have something to tell you about the fir trees of Oregon and the bamboos of my Fir Grove. Pat, he is my husband, you know, at last now you know, planted the bamboo trees for us, and they are nestled in our fir grove. The wind moves through the tall firs and the long bamboos in such a way that it is like a song, or rather a twin song, two murmuring voices that are answering each other.

The bamboo trees are tall now. They whisper in the light wind. In the evening, the sun plays among their leaves and canes. See them in this early evening light: touches of pale green, streaks of yellow, specks of brown, patches of dark and light. They have the rich tones of an Impressionist painting and the sobriety of a Japanese engraving. They are more beautiful than the sycamores by Lake Michigan's shores or the palm trees of the French Riviera by the blue Mediterranean waters. Pat often watches the bamboos at twilight, especially on an evening like this.

We're sitting outside on our patio. He turns to me with a twinkle in his eye and asks, "Darling, don't you think we can almost see the bamboo grow?"

Don't laugh because he calls me 'darling.' It may sound a bit old-fashioned, but the tenderness in his voice makes my heart melt. Yours would melt, too. How many of us can boast of having a husband who is as much in love with his wife after twenty-seven years of marriage as at the beginning? Pat always comments on the fast growth of the bamboos.

And I always answer, "Yes, indeed, I can see them grow; I can even hear them grow!" Pat laughs and I join in his laughter. I adore his chuckle of genuine amusement at my answer, always the same, responding to his familiar question.

Our State had a governor who recently became famous because he wanted tourists to visit Oregon and bring their tourist dollars but did not want them to stay. 'Don't Californicate Oregon,' was the popular slogan. Recent arrivals, yes, the people who had moved recently, became protective of their newly acquired life style and did not want others to join them. Does that make sense? In a country entirely based on immigration? Anyway, some Pacific North-Westerners don't appreciate newcomers.

If you really want to visit, come to my house, then. I will give you directions, just in case. My home is not too difficult to find if you pay attention. Let's assume you come from California. If you come from Alaska, reverse the directions. If you come from the West, or the East, by boat, by air, you can figure it out yourself, you are great travelers. So, from the South, head west, then make a slight turn, go straight and turn by the College. No, don't go toward the lake. Yes, I told you to avoid the cemeteries, both the Christian and Jewish one. Don't interrupt me all the time. We will make the graveyards larger soon enough. You do not appreciate my sense of humor? Well, you're just being overly sensitive. Anyway, back to directions. Head on straight a little while longer, roughly two miles.

Around the curve, splashes of sun contrast with the dark firs silhouetted against the sky. It is like entering a primeval forest. Here, in the West, even in the suburbs, you can feel exhilaration before the grandeur of nature and experience the fear of being alone. But, in fact, you are never alone.

Tall cedars, pines and firs crowd the edge of the road, hugging the bank. Driving toward the A-frame house, you will feel a sense of joy mixed with a shiver of apprehension. The house is hidden in the woods and can only be discovered at the end of the narrow, winding path which threatens to lose itself inside the forest. There. You've arrived. Do you catch a glimpse of the bamboo at the very edge of the wild garden? Probably not, you need to venture a little deeper into the front yard. Now, you are home.

Do you see us on the patio sipping our wine?

Good!

Our house is fairly new. Pat and I worked on our house plan for months. We had it built to our design. We knew we wanted lots of shelves for our books and shelving to the ceiling we got. I asked for a library ladder like the ones in British stately homes, and I have my rolling ladder. When it was new, I would perch myself on an upper step and Pat's eyes would twinkle as he admired my legs. Just like in a movie from the forties. Well, that's a story for another time. Let's not digress.

Pat does not need the ladder because he is so tall that he can reach most shelves, but I am on the petite side. In short, (not too clever a joke, you think, eternal smart aleck) the living room ended up looking like a library. Pat and I don't mind; on the contrary, that was our intent. A dining room, not too big, not too small, just right, like the bear's bed in Goldilocks (and the bowl and the chair before the bed, you say, pardon me!) Plus, a kitchen on a smaller scale. Have you noticed that the bigger the kitchen is, the less cooking gets done in it! It's just like spices, the more ostentatious the spice rack, the blander the food tastes in that particular, perfect house. At least, that's my theory.

We built two large bedrooms, a den and two bathrooms. It's handy to have large bedrooms since we are all untidy people and the large bedrooms are advantageous especially in these recent years when Pat has been bedridden so frequently. It is the perfect house for us. The terrace in the back was added some years later. We had to clear a bit of brush and cut down a few trees, which was a little sad but, in fact, the clearing for the terrace did a lot of good to the trees on the lot. Cutting some allowed more sun into the thicket and the remaining firs have shot up even higher.

Across from us, it is very quiet because there is a convent with a big dwelling hidden in eighteen acres of trees that are like a private wildlife refuge. When we moved in, two neighborly nuns came to introduce themselves and to ask all kinds of questions about our present habits (they knew a lot about habits) and future intentions (they knew less about intentions except God's.) Our answers must have been satisfactory, as they brought us a basket of treats: wine vinegar with a sprig of thyme floating in the bottle, blueberry jam, honey, and even a warm casserole, all homemade, not the honey, of course, bees made that! We became friends, even though Pat is an outspoken infidel. He has enjoyed many lively discussions on religious dogma with Sister Jeanne, the most intellectual of the sisters and he likes trying to catch her on particular points of theology.

The woods and our house are idyllic. But every bird needs to escape a gilded cage once in a while. I have loved to leave the nest, at times. Indeed, I have not left Rex, my son and Pat, my husband (you remember?) alone often. But, once in a while, I have the urge to get away. Pat understands perfectly. He is the one who first recognizes in me the signs of 'the call of the wild,' as he puts it. So, I plan a trip. Not alone; I wish I could. When I began my travels, it was not well thought of for a woman to travel alone, and it reassures Pat that I have a woman friend with me.

Before I married Pat, I did not go too far from Chicago and I did, occasionally, travel alone. I visited Minnesota, but that is another story altogether. What freedom I felt then! I still adore the smell of trains, the sight of railway cars passing by, smoke rising from the smokestack at twilight. My heart fills with yearning when I hear the lonely call of a train whistle in the night. In Chicago, our apartment was not far from a railroad station. As a child, I was lulled to sleep by the rumble of wheels on tracks and the shriek of brakes. I found comfort in what most people would have hated.

Arlo Guthrie just came out with a song about a train called "The City of New Orleans." I love the song; I can hear the clack, clack, clack of the wheels on the track and the whole feel evokes what I could not express to you.

Now, when I need to leave my little nest, I plan a trip with a woman friend and Pat works out the itinerary with us, beforehand. He is an avid reader and a great source of information. He checks ads in the newspapers and finds bargain prices on flights. He travels through me. From wherever I am, I write him a daily account of my adventures. He relishes my stories. Thus, the selected friend and I visit distant, warmer climes: California, Mexico, England (not warmer but exciting,) France, even Italy and Greece.

I would love to go to Japan (still his resentment from Pearl Harbor, you see), maybe Africa (too much de-colonization for him and fear of too many germs) but Pat has never been willing to see me go that far, particularly after a librarian from the University went to China alone and never came home. She contracted a very ordinary bug in a remote village and died at their poorly sanitized hospital. Since then, Pat does not want to hear about exotic destinations like Tahiti or Senegal, which are my idea of vacation paradises and where I would enjoy speaking French with the natives. Oh well, a married woman has to make some concessions to her mate. I don't want Pat to worry himself sick (he already is sick) about me since he is generous enough to let me go off on my own (with a friend.)

I am a little afraid of viruses myself, I don't know why. Wait, let's scratch that. My father died in 1946 of a virus in Spokane. Mother and I never knew the full details. He had been living in eastern Washington State with some shirttail relatives for nine years and was not doing well financially or otherwise. He had gone west in order to be a success. Go west young man, and grow up with the country... But it turned out Mother had to send him money often. And I did too, in secret, as soon as I could have a little job at the end of high school and during my college years. I loved my job at a florist shop, my senior year in high school. I learned about exotic flowers and I still have a soft spot for birds of paradise and orchids.

In college, I worked at the cafeteria, serving lunch to other students. I did not care much for that job, but I never had to worry about cooking for myself. I could eat all the food I wanted. Even today I don't like to cook everyday meals, although I love to prepare special dishes, mostly French and Spanish ones, for friends.

I adored my father when I was young. He was very dapper and when I was a little girl in Chicago, we would set off together on a Sunday afternoon, dressed impeccably, and take the tram to Lake Michigan 'to get out of Mother's hair.' We would stroll by the windy lake and watch the sailboats glide full speed over the water. Coming back home, he would buy me hard candy plus a small loaf of pumpernickel bread and talk about himself as a young man. From him came my love of the sea and faraway places. He would have been happier as a sailor than a lumberjack in Spokane, Washington.

On the other hand, Mother, who originally came from France (at least her mother did) always wanted to stay put. She had married quite late and then found herself stuck with her own mother living with us, crippled with rheumatism. Mother was raising me and had to work constantly, to make up for my father's irresponsibility. My father left us in 1936. It must have been in part to seek adventure, in part to escape Mother and Grandmother. Money was a convenient excuse, I think, now that I analyze the dynamics of my youth.

Mother and father were probably never well-suited as a couple but at that time there was not much one could do. Divorce was not an appropriate option for a proper family. I suppose the separation was a way for them to live independently without losing face. It was no wonder that Mother and Grandmother became bitter. Father ran away and escaped the reality of family, child rearing and responsibilities. Being such a handsome man, he must have had affairs. Most of the time Mother was close-mouthed, especially in front of me. I do remember heavy sighs from Grandmother's big bosom when my father was mentioned and I recall Mother's explanations in his defense, which, even then, sounded more like excuses.

Once in a while, at night when I was in bed, I remember Mother would talk to her mother, or in later years, over a glass of port, to my Aunt Minnie with whom we lived after my Grandmother died. She would let everything spill out like a dam overflowing. I would pretend to be asleep but I listened, holding my breath to hear every word. Mother poured out her 'truth' violently, spitefully, detailing Father's inadequate accomplishments and weak character. I can't imagine having to live with that anger, that sense of betrayal.

In contrast, my own marriage has been such a close relationship that I sometimes feel that Pat and I are like a real Janus, the twin-faced patron of the beginning and the end of things, one face looking at the rising sun and the other looking at the sunset.

2

KIMBERLEY'S JOURNAL
London

Tuesday morning, August 12, 1958

We slept till eight this morning. It was the first time in the week we've been here that both Carol and I have had a full night's sleep and we needed it. We've been setting quite a pace—and I've been lazy about my journal (but, God, London is great!) so I'm determined to get some of these adventures down on paper. As I look out, the August sun on Trafalgar Square promises a good day. We've had ideal weather: mostly clear but with a fresh breeze, so it hasn't been too hot. One day the temperature reached 75 degrees and the desk clerk commiserated with us about the excessive heat! I love this little old hotel, so pleasant and quiet and yet, situated between Trafalgar and Leicester Squares, really very convenient for our sightseeing forays.

Carol's stomach was upset last evening; it may have been the Bangers and Mash for dinner, but I hope that the night's rest will have her fit and frisky again, since we're planning to walk down the Thames Embankment to the Tower of London today. Carol is impatient with my dislike of public transport. She's a native of Chicago; her name was Judith originally, but she wants to be called Carole. Darn her, with her "e," like in Anne of the Green Gables. I call her Carol, with the normal Anglo-Saxon spelling of her middle name. Anyway, Carol is used to the bustle and press involved in buses. But I, having grown up in Oregon, neither like nor trust public conveyances. I always seem to be on the wrong one, going the wrong direction, and the crowds of people nauseate me. (God! Will the British ever adopt deodorants?)

When we walk, we can see everything and we're in total control of our destination. If I say so myself, I am **expert** at using a map, and given enough time I can get us anywhere. Carol would much prefer to stop and ask directions of any crone or urchin along the way. I suspect, too, that it's part of her pride in getting in touch with the natives—which I don't value as highly as she does. Just show me the Tower of London, the British Museum, St. Paul's—and get out of my way!

I was worried about Carol yesterday morning. She seemed to have no stamina and complained most of the day of a headache. I think the real reason for her malaise was that she hadn't heard from Pat, and considering his health problems, I know she must worry. I have to say, she's courageous and rarely mentions his difficulties or what they mean to her life. In fact, it couldn't have been easy for her to decide to come on this trip, especially after she spent two weeks of July in Chicago, trying to get her mother and aunt and their various doctors, clinics, diagnoses, and medications straightened out. She came back from that trip exhausted and embittered. Pat said he'd never seen her so downhearted.

She had apparently tried to get her mother into a special hospital using the old Chicago method: the brother of a friend's cousin knew the precinct captain and it was supposed to be a sure thing. It turned out not to be a sure thing and she found it terribly disillusioning. Carol's quite political, a diehard Democrat, and she grew up with considerable faith in the political structures in Chicago. Maybe because we've never had such an elaborate political machine on the West Coast, our great expectations are lower, and, consequently, our real disappointments are fewer. Anyway, when she returned to Portland in such a low frame of mind, Pat insisted that she come on this trip with me. He lives vicariously through her.

The three of us had planned it all last winter. We read volumes of British history in preparation and we had anticipated a great trip. Pat felt, rightly, I think, that this trip would be the antidote Carol needed for her Chicago experience. When we first arrived, Carol was thrilled, ecstatic. She kept saying, 'I adore London streets. I could walk in this city twenty-four hours a day.'

Considering how she has been relishing our travels, her low mood yesterday had me worried. Through these three or four years as teaching colleagues, I know her well enough to know that when she's up, she's very, very up—but when she's down, she's a pain in the ass. Yesterday we took a trip to Hampton Court, up the Thames. I did agree to go on that boat. I figured the boat had to be going in the right direction and we'd be out in the fresh air. We were able to board at Westminster Bridge for the five-hour trip upriver. The scenery along the summertime Thames was superb and we had a fine lunch, with some good English ale, on board ship. The royal apartments at Hampton Court were unbelievable and it was great to immerse ourselves in the 16th century atmosphere. In spite of the great trip, Carol seemed depressed all day.

For the downriver trip, the tide was going out and our return took only two hours. When we came back to the hotel, there was a letter from Pat and Carol was obviously delighted. Pat writes marvelous letters which Carol shares generously. I know she was relieved, too, to learn that their son Rex, who's only seven, seemed to be happy and enjoying the company of a new dog, Maverick. Carol had felt the dog was the last straw, with Pat's health so uncertain, Rex too young to take responsibility for a pet, and Carol herself having enough on her mind.

With her professional worries about the college's Foreign Language Department, which seems to get more chaotically political every term, and the personal burdens that go with being the mainstay and breadwinner of the family, she wasn't happy about adding another member to the family, even a well-behaved and intelligent standard poodle. In spite of her misgivings, it sounds as though the dog has been good for Rex, who, God love him, has had a tremendous amount of anxiety and uncertainty in his young life.

Pat's letter gave Carol a good laugh. He told her, among other things, that he was preparing a series of lectures for the Intervarsity Christian Fellowship entitled, "What Good Is Clean Fun?" I have to say, in spite of all their trials, it's hard not to envy what those two have. You'd never think they'd just celebrated their fifteenth anniversary. They have an intuitive communication and enjoyment of each other that you usually see only in very new relationships.

Knowing how close they are, I've been surprised at how much Carol travels without Pat, but since he's so often either in the hospital or very low physically, in a way, I guess she travels for them both. I remember her telling of a car trip she took to Mexico with three friends from her college days, all women. This was about five years ago, in 1953. It wasn't long before Carol and Pat moved to the Northwest but at that time they were still living in Chicago. These four women drove from Chicago down through Missouri to New Orleans, then across Texas to Brownsville where they crossed the border into Mexico. Carol said it was astonishingly foreign: women in their black shawls and bare feet, men wearing guns in those wild border towns. I can imagine the impact on four American school teachers from the Midwest.

A few miles south of the Border they took a short cut. A man had told Carol of a road, recently finished, which would save them seventy-five miles on their way to the main highway to Mexico City. They found themselves on a primitive road through the cactus and rock-strewn desert of northern Mexico. They drove for two hours without seeing another car, wondering if their twice-repaired tires would hold. Now that is intrepid traveling! In spite of some nervous moments and upset stomachs, they made their way safely to Mexico City where the tourist life was dirt cheap; three or four dollars would cover hotel and food for the day.

Carol was the group's translator. I know she grew up in a French family, but she has also studied and taught Spanish and Portuguese over the years and I suppose fluency in one language aids fluency in others. Hard for us monolingual English Literature teachers to understand. I must say, her descriptions of the bougainvillea-draped homes in Cuernavaca and the little mountainside hotel in Taxco, overlooking cathedral, plaza and market place, almost made me want to visit Mexico. Almost.

Speaking of sightseeing, I must rouse my partner now so that we can get down to the breakfast room before it closes at nine. Carol was so keyed up after getting Pat's letter last night that, in spite of her upset stomach, she took a couple of sleeping pills to settle down. She'll be groggy for a while this morning. I sometimes wonder if she has as much respect for self-medication as she should, but I keep my counsel. The generous English breakfast with fried everything is good, if a bit hard on the waistline. We are served with great correctness by an ancient maid who looks as though she stepped right out of *The Forsyte Saga* and the cozy breakfast room with its chintz curtains puts us in just the proper frame of mind for the day.

Wednesday, August 13

Yesterday was quite a day. We were gone from 9:45 a.m. until 10:30 last evening. In the morning, we walked down the Thames embankment toward the Tower of London. We had been told of a pub within the enclosure of

'The Ivory House' which used to be the East India Trading Company. We did manage to find it and have lunch there. Gigantic ivory elephants top the gateposts and the whole place reeks of imperial times when Britannia ruled the waves. We were the only tourists in the place. It was filled with serious naval officers. Carol, as is her way, struck up a conversation with a good-looking Navy Captain who told us about the history of the place. British people always seem surprised at how interested Carol and I are in English history and how much we know. Their surprise doesn't say much for the level of ignorance they encounter in the average American tourist.

I'm always amused watching Carol when she meets an attractive man. Her whole demeanor changes. She can be so haughty and cold with, for example, an arrogant waiter. Get her into conversation with someone like the naval captain and there's a transformation. With her lovely smile and infectious laugh, including a funny little concluding snort, she tells a story so vividly that by the end of the tale the listener is captivated. The naval captain was and clearly would have liked to extend the acquaintance, but Carol can extricate herself as deftly as she can draw a new person in. We escaped the smitten captain in time to finish our afternoon at the Tower.

For supper, we went to another pub, The Mermaid, where I hit it off with the Irish waitress. When I ordered my third Scotch, just to take the edge off the day, she beamed. "You're a girl after me own heart!"

I had a steak, a bit tougher here than at home, but I think they have more real beef flavor. Carol had a pint of bitter. God! Who would drink that stuff when you could have a Scotch? And she ordered Lancashire tripe. It must be the French in her that made that sound appealing. I didn't even want to look at it and kept my eyes on my beefsteak.

Our after-dinner escapade perfectly illustrates travel with Carol. We were to go to the theater and, according to my map, we were very near it. However, between The Mermaid and the theater lay a Great Gulf Fixed: a freeway and a five-foot fence. Carol insisted we climb the fence. It must have been the after-dinner Drambuie. The fence was nearly as tall as we were, but she was halfway up it before I could marshal my arguments. I could either stand there and scream at her or follow her over the fence.

We did make it over the fence with minimum damage to our clothing and the complete destruction of our dignity. We were giggling like two silly teenagers instead of two middle-aged women who should know better. By the grace of God and London highway engineers, on the other side of the fence there was a pedestrian overpass to get us across the freeway, so at least we didn't have to take on the rush hour traffic, which I think Carol would have done, too!

One night last week, she had a vodka and a scotch before we went out for dinner and she was, as she said, 'so bouncy' that she crossed Piccadilly in front of the oncoming red double-decker buses and all the taxi cabs by setting her jaw, thrusting up her left hand in a clenched, defiant gesture, and marching through the middle of the traffic, with me trailing nervously behind.

The play last evening was a new one with John Gielgud in the lead. I had hoped we could see him in one of the great Shakespearean roles, but August isn't the best season for theater, so you take what you can get. The London theaters deserve their excellent reputation: we've seen four productions in our ten days here and all have been first-rate. The tickets are ridiculously cheap. If you sit up in 'the gods,' admission is a pittance. We feel justified in leaving those seats to the penniless students and treating ourselves to front first balcony seats, which are ideal. The tickets run us only a pound or two. The theaters are really still in their first flush of their revival after the difficulties of the early postwar years, so there's a definite feeling of renaissance.

Carol is a great theater-going partner. She doesn't have my background in British literature, but she's widely read and certainly has a fine mind. We have the after-theater habit of stopping for a drink on the way back to the hotel, which gives us the opportunity to discuss what we've just seen. Sometimes our discussions get fairly intense, but just when I'm getting heated up over some point, Carol will switch to her non-committal mode: "*Really.*" She'll say, "Do you *think* so? Hmm. Did you see that blonde over in the corner? I'm sure she's trying to charm that young man out of his family's fortune." The wind is out of my sails, the subject is safely changed, and the good will of our traveling partnership is restored.

I'm on my way out to the Tate Gallery now. Carol refuses. She insists on spending a morning in department stores, for God's sake. We'll meet for lunch at a pub not too far from Windsor Castle and then go to the Changing of the Guard.

Thursday, August 14

Great afternoon yesterday. In the morning, I may have set some kind of record for getting through the entire exhibition at the Tate in about two hours. I think many of the paintings are rather mediocre, especially the more modern ones. Trashy. The Constables are wonderful, though. I could spend a day just with them. Carol and I met at a pub, the Red Rabbit, for lunch. An Irish gypsy insisted on telling Carol's fortune using Tarot cards but when Carol asked about her son, Rex, the gypsy closed the session abruptly, insisting that she could not read the future of a person who wasn't there. I thought she looked suddenly sad, but perhaps I was imagining things. I'm sure she was as much of a charlatan as all her sister fortune tellers.

Carol was gaga about the department stores she'd seen on her morning's expedition, loved them all, but especially

Harrods'. Marshall Field's (the big Chicago outfit) is like Woolworth's compared to Harrods's, she assured me. There was one whole room devoted to picnic baskets outfitted elaborately with crystal, silver, stainless steel thermoses, etc. She found the display enchanting and was wishing Pat could have seen it.

After lunch, we walked up to Buckingham Palace for the Changing of the Guard. It was hard to see with crowds of taller people in front of us. Carol hoisted herself up on a six-foot fence and was delighted with the view. I was aghast. Sometimes Carol's lack of decorum makes being her travel partner rather trying. But she just shrugs and points out that this may be the only chance she ever has to see something and she damned well isn't going to miss it. I believe that a person's dignity should not be sacrificed entirely no matter what the temptation. Carol, of course, had an unobstructed full-length view of the guards in their dramatic uniforms, while I had to catch glimpses between shoulders and heads of other tourists.

We visited the Houses of Parliament in the late afternoon. One of the guards was especially accommodating. He opened a case and let Carol and I read actual documents from Cromwell's time. We get a great deal of information from the people who work in these places. Once they know we are genuinely interested, they tell us fascinating things that we would, otherwise, never learn.

After Parliament, we repaired to the Swiss Tourist Centre for our dinner. The restaurant there serves desserts that can only be described as beatific: all that Swiss chocolate with whipped cream! I find the place a little annoying: the manager and waiters practically refuse to speak English. And everyone knows the Swiss speak excellent English! Of course, Carol loves this as she can flirt with them all in French. It's embarrassing how they fawn over her and call her *mon amour*. It gets a little old after a while. The food, however, is excellent and reasonably priced, and it's conveniently near our hotel, so I keep quiet.

I'm curious about this flirtatiousness of Carol's. I wonder if it ever comes to anything. Obviously not when she and I are traveling together, but what about when she's on her own. I think of her stories of last summer when she took an extended summer session at Berkeley and Pat and Rex stayed home in Portland. Carol missed them terribly and told me how lonely and distraught she was. Pat's frequent letters were all that saved her. (An example: when she had nineteen days left, and had sounded in very low spirits over the phone, Pat sent her nineteen postcards with funny little messages and sketches to cheer her up.)

I also remember her telling of visiting the Stanford Foreign Language Department to investigate their Ph.D. program in the company of a classmate from Berkeley. This was an all-day expedition, and he was, as she described him, the charming scion of old California money. They finished up in a jazz club in San Francisco on a lovely summer evening. You can't help but wonder if they really finished up at the jazz club!

I think of stories like that when I see the coquette emerge to flirt with the waiters in the Swiss Centre restaurant.

Which reminds me that I'm also curious about this Ph.D. business. Carol, for all her talkativeness, has that French discretion, foreign to us Western Americans; so even after these years as colleagues, there are many things that I don't know about her background. For example, I had assumed from some conversations that the work at Berkeley was in partial fulfillment of Ph.D. requirements, but if she really had started a doctorate there, I don't think she would have been checking out the Stanford program. I suppose she's like me and many other women: bogged down and boggle-minded from the effort required to teach college courses full time, run a household, and still try to figure out how to pursue a higher degree.

Her M.A. from the University of Chicago got her the job at Meriwether University and her brilliance and teaching skills have kept her there. We both know, if you're going to stay in college teaching and prosper, you had better get those three letters, Ph.D., after your name.

Speaking of Carol as a teacher reminds me of a story a young student told me last winter. The student, Gayle, a bright if naïve girl, was enrolled in Carol's First-year French class which met just before she came to my Survey of English Lit. Gayle came in, one gloomy January morning, looking very upset. I like to try to get to know my freshmen students, especially the young women who show promise and need encouragement, so I made some tentative inquiries.

It turned out that in the middle of the French class, one of the other students had tossed a used Kleenex into the wastebasket beside Carol's desk. Carol was furious and launched into a scathing sermon; first she covered what the girl ought to have done with the tissue (taken it and its germs home and disposed of it in the bathroom) and then she moved on to an explication of the distinction the French make between *instruction*, or book-learning, which this class was imparting, and *education*, which I suppose is close to what we refer to as being well-bred, and which the unfortunate girl and her Kleenex clearly were not. Gayle said that this sermon was delivered with a cold scorn which was completely humiliating, and if she had been its target, she could never have returned to that class.

I found this incident intriguing if not shocking. I know Carol prides herself on maintaining control over her class by an assumed iciness. I've seen her use that coldness on headwaiters and hapless train station clerks, but I've never seen her go into a temper such as Gayle described. I wonder if she does it at home. That could explain some of the nervousness I see in little Rex, who clearly adores his mother. I had always attributed the child's emotional fragility to the unpredictability of Pat's health and the inconsistent child-care arrangements that inevitably result. I have a feeling Carol would never let that temper loose on Pat, though. There is, for all the humor and affection, a core of steel in him. He would not tolerate being attacked by a shrewish wife and Carol's smart enough to know it.

In spite of that story, it's only fair to say that Carol's students, including Gayle, adore her. She always has a little contingent of moon-eyed freshmen at her door during office hours and she's generous with both her time and attention. One of the college's bright young student politicians seemed promising but provincial to Carol, so she sent him a subscription to 'The New Yorker.'

Gayle also told me that once when she was working in the student bookstore, Carol came in. Gayle showed her a handsome new **History of France** by Maurois. Carol bought it, paid for it and then handed it to Gayle as a gift, saying laughingly, "You need this. You are **terribly** ignorant of French history!" Such generosity to students and friends is certainly one of Carol's most endearing characteristics.

Ooouf. Time to head for bed if I'm to be ready for our last day of London sightseeing.

Friday, August 15

Since we'll be leaving for Paris tomorrow morning, we have been taking care of a couple of necessary errands yesterday and today. For one thing, early yesterday morning Carol insisted we go to Liverpool Station to make our train/boat reservations for next week. We'll be taking the train to Bournemouth and then a boat across the English Channel to France.

From Liverpool Station, I agreed to take the Green Line underground to Windsor. We were lucky enough to catch an express, which was not very crowded at that hour and we arrived in Windsor by 9 a.m. 'Rush hour' here is about an hour later than at home and since we're used to rising early, that's to our advantage. The weather has turned surprisingly cold and Carol had been chilled on the way to Windsor. She has adopted the British—I guess it's European—custom of wearing no hose in the summer time. It's shocking to me. And in a travel-friendly nylon dress, she was not dressed warmly enough. I was in a double-knit wool suit under my London Fog raincoat, with stockings and I was reasonably comfortable.

Anyway, she insisted that she was chilled to the bone, so we stopped in a pub for a whiskey, and then, guidebooks in hand, went carefully through about half the castle, by which time we were ready for lunch. We found an excellent pub on High Street patronized by well-bred, well-dressed, apparently well-heeled businessmen. Carol was in her element. All those slim, suave, nicely tailored gentlemen. We agreed: when we see a slob, he's probably American!

Today I had promised I'd go with Carol to Kew Gardens. Pat is quite a gardener; he's done some nice things on their little suburban lot. Gardening is one thing he can do. During his lower times, he can plot and plan and then when he's feeling stronger, he can putter around in the yard. Pat has read about famous gardens and he insisted that Carol mustn't miss this opportunity to visit Kew. Earlier last week the weather was lovely; we should have gone then. I guess we're used to long spells of pleasant weather in the summer and we assumed it would last, but yesterday and today there has been a cold, leaden sky with a nasty breeze. Even so, we set off in good time this morning by bus for Richmond, where Kew Gardens are located. We thought the 288 acres were beyond us, so we concentrated on the historical plantings and the Bamboo Garden. Pat has a particular enthusiasm for bamboo and he had made us promise that we would bring him back a report on that section.

Carol has more than once quoted a letter in which he had written her 'when you are gone, the summer breeze is just wind and the bamboo is just another plant.' I enjoyed looking up a list of plants mentioned in the writings of Shakespeare. Since they are mostly annuals or rapidly-growing perennials, they have been fairly easy to restore to their previous splendor after the years of wartime neglect.

The bamboo garden was another thing. Having been neglected through most of the 1940's for lack of manpower and through the 50's for lack of funds, the garden had done what you would expect a bamboo garden to do: run amok. The Kew people are in the midst of a complete renovation: digging out overgrown plants and restoring order to the plantings. In another year or two the bamboo section will be lovely again.

There is something about the combination of delicacy and strength in bamboo, the tactile qualities of the smooth and neatly sectioned trunks, the whisper of the papery leaves that draw you to it. The condition of the garden was a reminder that beauty is enhanced by discipline, and lack of order can spoil it. Which puts me in mind of some of the creative writing I see from my college freshmen!

By early afternoon, we had had our fill of Kew and I persuaded Carol that she must visit the Tate Gallery with me even if briefly, promising her rooms of luminous Constables as her reward. It was not a good decision as it led to the most upsetting scene of our entire London trip and I fear it will color our memory of London. When we entered the Tate, Carol had to check her camera.

This camera has been a standing joke with us. She borrowed it from a friend. She had misgivings about taking it, but he insisted that she do so in order to bring photos home to Pat and Rex. She finally agreed when she learned that I was not planning to bring a camera but preferred instead to write a journal and purchase guidebooks. Carol is, among her friends, notorious for her ineptitude with any kind of technology: film projectors, tape recorders. Any machinery reduces her to trembling incompetence. Not only is she nervous when she's using the camera, many times she hasn't even had it along on sightseeing trips, having inadvertently left it behind in the hotel room.

We agree that it is undoubtedly her subconscious taking over and that she'll be lucky if she doesn't leave the camera on a bus seat, a thought that terrifies her since she feels so responsible for getting Winston's camera back to him. She had brought the camera out for the Kew trip so that she could record the Bamboo Garden for Pat. It was with us when we entered the Tate and she was required to check it, as is common in most of the museums.

When we were leaving the Tate after a fairly short visit, we picked up the camera. She looked at it and was convinced that it was not the same camera. They had switched cameras on her. She accused the young man in the checkroom. He was, of course, highly offended, denied it vehemently and she backed down. We went out the front door. On the steps outside she insisted he had switched it.

"This is not Winston's camera. I know it's not!" And stormed back in. By this time, I was wondering why in the name of God there was no kind of name tag, label, or identification on the camera, but apparently, she had never put one on, nor had Winston.

Again, the young man, this time supported by a middle-aged female colleague, insisted that it was **certainly** the same camera. Carol retreated again, at my insistence. Out on the steps once more, she kept looking at the camera, noticing knobs and buttons she'd never seen before, or never noticed before.

I could be of no help. I had never looked at the damned camera. Back into the museum she went, one more time. This time, the manager joined the fray and when Carol reiterated her claim that the camera had been switched: the camera she'd brought in had **not** had that particular knob;

he asserted coldly that there could not possibly have been a mistake and began to hint darkly about calling the police to settle the matter.

The threat of actual police involvement finally caused Carol to subside. As we beat an embarrassed and unhappy retreat, she moaned, "Well, if this isn't Winston's camera, he can just come to London himself and get the wretched thing back!"

Carol was terribly upset over this episode, which was, of course, of her own making. A simple name tag on the camera would have prevented the entire problem and made the whole exhausting scene unnecessary, but I didn't have the heart to state the obvious. In my heart of hearts, I believed the British attendant, not Carol. We retreated to The Pastoria and my bottle of Scotch. Fortunately, a cheerful letter from Pat, reporting all was well with himself, Rex and the dog, awaited Carol at the hotel.

Carol went to bed early tonight. Says she has blisters on every toe. Well, for that matter, so do I. But she does seem really fatigued and continues to complain about dizziness. The restaurant where we had dinner, after we had recovered somewhat from 'The Incident of the Camera,' prided itself on its roast beef. Our dinner consisted of huge servings of the house specialty and we topped off the meal with cheesecake, served British style, with mounds of whipped cream.

I have a cast-iron stomach, myself, and all that rich food suited me just fine. Carol's system is more delicate, however. Perhaps she's having that French complaint: is it *crise de foie?* Well, she'd better get over her French complaint and into her French mode, as we're off to Paris in the morning.

I do hope the memory of the silly camera business will fade quickly as we have had a wonderful stay here in England and I'd hate to have a shadow cast over our recollections of this time in London.

Now, with Carol returning to her homeland, I'm hopeful that Paris will be even better. Off to pack the faithful American 'Tourister' in order to be ready for an early start.

3

MERIWETHER UNIVERSITY
Winter Term, 1975, in the morning

"You didn't forget, Gustav? She's called for a Departmental meeting this afternoon, at three. I hope you'll be there." Enrico Vicenti, Professor of Italian, said as he stopped his German colleague passing in front of his open door.

"I will be there, of course." Gustav Baum answered, straightening his books and notes that he had slipped under his arm.

Enrico went on, whispering this time, "Good. Do you have a minute? We should brainstorm if we want to be ready to counteract her farfetched schemes. Come in my office. You know how she is!"

SHE, naturally, was Carole (with an 'e') Murray, Professor of French and the current Chair of the Foreign Languages Department, their common enemy of the moment.

"Don't remind me. She is weird! You know what? After the accusations that flew around at the last meeting, I think I should bring a tape recorder for this afternoon. This way, no one can claim later that he or she did not say what we know he or she said at the meeting. What do you think? Brilliant, eh?"

"Hey, great idea! That will make her see red and she'll lose her cool, the icy queen."

"You want to hire that young instructor in Italian and I'd like to ask for one more position in German. Let's not pussyfoot around any longer. It's getting serious."

"She's never going to agree about new hires in Italian and German. They desperately need someone in French. That will be her priority. Forget about us. She has two years left as Department Chair. How can we stand it that much longer?"

"Besides, I'll bet she'll want to hire women. All those females have banded together. They're claiming they don't make as much money as we do."

"As if theirs were real careers! They've got husbands and boyfriends to support them. They're even threatening to file a class action suit with the State. That's all we need."

"Next they'll want to have their place kept on hold while they're out there having babies."

"You know what she implied about her wish list for changes in personnel policy! Women should even be paid for a month after the birth of a baby. That will never happen. Apparently, our Carol has proposed to emulate the French with their stupid socialized medicine."

"As usual, we men will be left holding the bag. Mark my words, one of these days we'll have to accept them teaching with a crying brat at their hips and babies in departmental meetings."

"You remember old Lenox, the Dean who retired several years ago, so different from our present one, Dean Luponski. Well, Lenox was Murray's mentor. He was our poet in residence and later, became Dean. Thank God, he finally retired."

"I still wonder how he became Dean, with no administrative skills whatsoever."

"True. He helped hire Carol because they were both from Chicago."

"I never knew old Lenox's whole story."

"I met a guy who worked with him when he was at the University of Chicago. This guy assumed I was on Lenox's side and part of his team. He poured his guts out to me! It seems Lenox fought in France in WWI, then came back and married a young chick who taught at Northwestern. There was a clause against nepotism. They never told anyone they were married then, because she would have been fired."

"That's pretty devious, hiding his marriage for her to get a job at the same university. Don't you think it's deceitful?"

"Of course, it is. Anyway, both of them hid the marriage from everyone. What they would do, in fact, is to slip away to England and France every summer together. Because of his secretive life, some colleagues became suspicious of Lenox."

"Who wouldn't have been, with him obviously leading a double life?"

"Suspicions were directed at Lenox's politics, and one day he was called in. They asked him, 'Have you ever been a member of the Communist Party?' He wouldn't answer, on principle, that's what he claimed. What a joke! Anyway, he was fired. This was when he was still back in Chicago. Later, he told his friends that he had no use for Communism but he would definitely refuse to answer such questions."

"How stupid of him! Why didn't he tell the committee the truth?"

"Anyway, that's when he was fired, he came west and was snapped up by the Linguistics Department at Berkeley. He brought his wife along openly this time."

"Oh, they mustn't have a rule forbidding two married profs in the same school."

"No. Then he was hit by McCarthyism again and was fired once more. Somehow, in all his wanderings, he had met someone from Meriwether University and that's how we ended up inheriting him as poet in residence and then Dean, plus his wife too!"

"I think his poetry is like milk toast, myself. And we are stuck with his wife teaching English Lit., in evening classes. Talk about nepotism!"

"That's when he hired young Carol, fresh from the Windy City. Lenox created a post just for Professor Carol Murray. And we've had her on our backs since."

"I don't know what we can do. She's pretty much entrenched. Anyway, I need to run to class, I'll be late. See you at three. Ciao."

Professor Gustav Baum rushed to his classroom, slightly late as usual, the smell of his tobacco pipe pervading the long corridor. He was ready to lecture on Goethe. He had just finished polishing an article on an unknown figure among Goethe's friends, of which he was very proud.

Same day. 5:00 p.m.

Enrico Vicenti took his jacket from his coat rack and slipped it on, ready to leave, when Gustav Baum passed again in front of his office door.

"Here you are, Gustav," Enrico said, a grin on his face. "What a meeting! Boy, was she furious when she walked in and saw the tape recorder on the table! Did you see her chin start to quiver? She's clever. She never said anything. In fact, I thought her voice became even sweeter. Still, I caught her icy glare. It gave me the chills."

"Yea, she never asked who had put the tape-recorder there before the meeting." The German professor answered, a big smile on his face, "But when the recorder stopped in the middle of the session, I was the one who put a fresh blank tape in. She wasn't going to take advantage of that and manipulate me further."

"She's off her rocker. I wonder if she's on antidepressants or has one drink too many regularly. She must drink at home with her invalid of a husband."

"She did remain calm though her authority was being questioned, obviously. Anyone else would have blown up. She didn't flinch after the initial shock."

"Did you see all the weaklings around the room, not daring to speak because the recorder was on?"

"Half of them have no balls." They both chuckled.

"That's why she got elected in the first place. Thanks to those weaklings. Mediocrity wins. Beware of still waters, I always say."

"Oh, I've got to tell you. I found out some more about our Professor Carol Murray from a friend of mine in Illinois. He called me at noon. Out of mere curiosity, I had told him to check out her family history and her school stories. She always says she didn't finish her Ph.D. at the University of Illinois because of her husband's illness. But she was not married then and, apparently, she never was enrolled in a Ph.D. program, at all. Do you believe this?"

"The deceitful bitch!"

"She received her B.A. from St. Teresa College, and her M.A. from the University of Chicago, that's true. That's what she has on her resume. But after teaching in a couple of high schools in Illinois during World War II, there's a gap. That's when she was supposed to be at the University of Illinois. No way, Jose, according to my well-informed source."

"Well, this is interesting. Curiouser and curiouser."

"That gap of time after Sherman High School is just mystery number one."

"And mystery number two? Come on, tell me."

"In 1947, she was teaching at Loyola College in Chicago. In all her teaching jobs, she taught French and Spanish, even some Portuguese and English at the beginning. Then she shows up in Washington State or Oregon at the end of the '49 summer. She arrives here brandishing her Chicago sophistication, her genetic Frenchness and her air of intellectual superiority."

"OK, but get to the point. What's mystery number two?"

"I am to the point. My friend met someone who went to grade school with Carol with no 'e.' I think she's not French at all. She was raised in a poor suburban area of Chicago. She was born Judith, Carol Jensen and then became the wife of Patrick John Murray. Does any of that sound French?"

"Well, it could be on her mother's side."

"I doubt it. I heard the mother is from Minnesota and the dad worked in the mines. He was a logger for a while in Spokane, Washington, leaving the family behind in Chicago. That's what my friend said. Pretty blue collar, eh?"

"I knew it. And she pretends to be high class. You know what Juan Garcia told me the other day about Carole's summer trip to France. She came back from Paris through London and was searched by the British customs. She had French cheeses hidden in various pockets."

A woman custom officer searched her and, apparently, told her, "It's a good thing I'm in a good mood today, Madam, otherwise you would be in big trouble!" Murray managed to talk the female official into letting her keep the cheeses without a fine because she missed them 'sooo muuuch' in the U.S., where all American cheeses are orange in color and taste like wax. Blah, blah, blah. What gall that woman has!"

"What nerve, alright. See, you have our modern society now: in England, they have female custom officers and here we have a chairwoman. She's so proud to be the first woman chair here at the University! Big deal. I don't even know what to call her, Madame Chairman, Madame Chairwoman, Ms. Murray, Mrs. Chair, Carol, Carole with an 'e' or what. What about Charwoman?"

"Charwoman, that's good! She told Juan, 'I am a woman, not a piece of furniture.' I guess that means she doesn't fancy being called 'Chair.' I'm going to call her 'Miiiizzzz Chair' next time, just to annoy her."

"I'm sure she's been instrumental in starting that discrimination suit and affirmative action crap. We've got to make sure she doesn't get elected again!"

"We will, when it's time. OK. I need to run. Bye."

"So long... See you tomorrow."

The two men went their separate ways, Enrico Vicenti closing his office door behind him and turning left toward the garage building, and the other, Gustav Baum, turning right at the end of the corridor to grab his coat in his office.

4

ON CAMPUS
Spring Term 1975

It was a bright, sunny spring afternoon where soft tendrils of shade played with narrow shafts of light. Green buds were already bursting into leaves on the oak trees. What a waste to have to work inside one's small office on campus. Sue Gale, Professor of English, went to the phone to call Fanny Taylor, Professor of French. They were good friends and colleagues of Professor Carol Murray, head of the Foreign Language Department and Fanny's boss.

"Can we get together to have a cup of coffee somewhere instead of being confined inside?" asked Sue.

"Great idea. See you at the cafeteria, right now."

Sue bought her cafeteria coffee and made a face as she swallowed a sip of the weak brew. She sighed when Fanny arrived. "That coffee is just like warm water. We need to do something about it." Sue complained, taking another sip. "Well. Did you see the newspaper today? When I opened the 'Living Section' whom did I see? Our friend, Enrico. There's a big picture of him with a wide smile, a cigarette between his fingers, in front of a crowd of students, a self-satisfied look on his face. I could not believe his posturing! The article talked about him teaching a new class in Italian using a revolutionary 'active method.' How can people fall for this guy's self-promotion? Even I, an English professor, know that's nothing new. The article made the method sound brand-new and of Enrico's invention."

Fanny carried her cup of coffee to a table, out of habit, changed her mind and, turning to Sue said, "No, I haven't seen the article. Let's go outside and sit on a bench. The weather is too good to stay indoors. When I passed Stafford Hall last week, I saw a crowd in front of Enrico's class. A cameraman and a journalist stood close by. I assumed he had called the media."

"The article talks of 'using the target language' to conduct this new style of classes. The difference is that some of us know how to promote ourselves and some don't. Have you ever wondered why most chefs are men? Their mothers and grandmothers cooked all their lives but men appropriated their recipes and publicized them. *C'est la vie!* You and I are not good businesswomen."

"I am just as glad; I find all that self-aggrandizement demeaning. Perhaps, we should do a better job at selling our goods of the mind or, one day, we'll find ourselves relegated to the category of dinosaurs."

"That may be. Who has time to be both teacher and public relations agent? Not me. With teaching, running a house, kids, publishing and the rest of it? It's a 70-hour job."

"We sound bad, you know! Think of the poor women and children working in the mines in nineteenth-century England or nowadays in African or India or even here!"

"I know, you're right. But we can still complain to our friends once in a while, can't we?" They both laughed and sat down on an outside bench in the sun. Their legs extended in front of them, they let the sun shine on their shins.

"Of course, *chérie*. Isn't that why we are such good friends, besides our parallel situations and the fact that we are both so kind and so intelligent?" They giggled again, enjoying the warmth of the sun.

"You'd better stop with the compliments. You know what we say in French. *Arrête les compliments ou tu vas te faire une bosse avec le pot !* Stop throwing flowers at me, or else you'll have a lump on the head from the flowerpot. Stupid expression, but I love it."

"Cute! Hey, I meant to tell you what happened last week with your boss Carol, and with Dick Doyle, the head of the

International Program. I heard it straight from the horse's mouth. One afternoon after the Senate meeting, Carol went to Dick's office for another meeting of the International Program Committee; they're both members. The committee met in Dick's office, which is quite large. She saw his Portuguese dictionary open on the desk. She began speaking Portuguese to him, for fun, and he kept answering 'si, si''and that's all. She did not know, but apparently, his command of the language is not good at all, in spite of his bragging. I guess he was a little embarrassed. Carol's Spanish and Portuguese are very good. Carol did not mean to intimidate him with her language abilities, but he was intimidated all the same."

"Later, in the committee meeting, Dick was going on at length about how important it was for students to study languages and international subjects and how great it was to have our student program abroad. He wanted to ingratiate himself once more to the committee, I suppose. He was certain Carol would agree with him. Instead, she said he had it all wrong and that students should be studying courses that would teach them how to live first, especially how to navigate life in large cities, before they were sent to Europe."

"He must've been astonished."

"He was. She went on to say that one should not put the cart before the horse. Some of the country kids at the university should have more urban survival skills before they learned international skills, and before they were sent abroad, totally naïve, like lambs to the slaughter."

"Dick was the slaughtered lamb, in that case!"

She went on to say, "Some of our eighteen-year-old who are forbidden by law to drink at home, stayed drunk for three weeks straight when they arrived in France, buying big jugs of red wine. Then they emerged from their alcoholic trance to go to their classes at the French university. The Professors in France were appalled by the American students' behavior. One of them shouted, 'If young people can drive a car and go to war - in Vietnam nowadays, you not having learned anything from the French in Indochina and the Dien Bien Phu fiasco - then those students should be able to learn how to drink and know their limits before the age of twenty-one.' That was unfair but still somewhat true."

Sue sighed.

"There was silence in the room and Dick was dumfounded. He was upset that she had questioned his good sense in front of the whole group."

"What happened then?"

"After the meeting, Carol asked Dick if he could give her a ride home since they live in the same neighborhood. Her car was in the garage. He agreed to give her a ride. Then his old Toyota started acting up. To his great embarrassment, he had to ask her to sit in the driver's seat and push the starter while he manipulated the carburetor to make the damned thing start. Carol thought the whole incident hilarious and laughed through it all with great glee. But he was mortified and now, by retelling the story, she lets others know that he drives a junk car. Some people think Carol is a snob. In fact, she is able to enjoy the moment and life's surprising twists and turns. I don't think she realized that Dick was embarrassed. Anyway, the darned car started and they both got home safely. That's all there is to the story, but I thought it was funny."

"Yes. That's totally Carol, isn't it? That's how she reacts. Did you ever hear the story about when she was in college and met the French writer Jules Romains?"

"No. How did that one go?"

"Well, it was back in 1940, when she was young, in Chicago. Apparently, Jules Romains was invited for a conference on his work or something like that. There was a reading of his famous play, *Knock or the Triumph of Medicine*, which is filled with parody and humor. Carol always thought the play was funny. She likes anything medical and she knows quite a bit about Romains' theory of 'unanism.' She agreed with his comments about problems of conscience in modern society. His essays do raise the question of complexity within contemporary life and that was quite new back then.

"I see, probably at its peak in the U.S. when Carol was in college."

"Somehow, she succeeded in being invited to act as his guide and translator; I don't know how. She ended up attending every event and providing entertainment for him and his wife. There was a festive dinner and Carol happened to sit next to Jules Romains's wife. The only thing she had to say after the experience was that Romains was indeed a good writer with a social conscience but that the man himself was ordinary. Moreover, she let it be known what she thought of his wife."

"What about the wife?"

"She said that Romains's wife was just about the most vulgar woman she'd ever met. I don't know how it happened, but the words were repeated to Romains; he and his wife left in a huff, shunning Carol who was the butt of jokes among her fellow students for several months afterwards."

"It must have given her a reputation for being truthful to a fault!"

"Totally! Good or bad, a reputation all the same. Carol was pleased."

"I don't know if Carol is too truthful or a real snob! That's part of her mystery and her charm."

"Yes. Can't you see her as a young college woman, so petite, pretty, bright and funny, with that hourglass figure of hers? All the same, behind the charming smile and laughter, I suspect there's a hidden side to her personality that no one knows, except perhaps her husband and son."

"Her life is so sad at home with Pat very ill most of the time. She certainly knows first-hand the irony inherent in life's contradictions and setbacks. And she manages to smile in spite of it all. I think that's what I admire about her the most: her resilience."

"By the way, not to change the subject, but we'd better not have a setback ourselves. We need to get together to outline that article we talked about on Wordsworth and the influence of the French Revolution on his ideas. We must get it written and out soon, or someone else will use that material those Scottish scholars uncovered last year. Plenty has been written, but I think we have a fresh angle. Besides, it would be good for our tenure, wouldn't it?"

"You're right. But I've been swamped. I'm coordinating the teaching of all the lower division classes on top of teaching my normal courses, and it's taken quite a bit of my extra time along with getting quizzes and tests ready and correcting papers. Let's meet this Sunday at your house at 9 a.m. We'll send our husbands to the park with the kids and dogs! We can make a nice pot of coffee, real coffee, and I'll bring the croissants."

"Deal, Sunday it is. By the way, everyone in the English Department is talking about the rift within your Foreign Language Department. Carol is having problems with your macho men because of the Affirmative Action suit. Wasn't it great that we won? Do you realize it's going to add almost $1,000 to our pay check next year to come to parity with the men in equivalent positions? It might even be spread over several years, perhaps. There will be differences, of course, because of merit increase and so on, but what a victory!"

"It's fantastic. That's why I've become the coordinator instead of Bill, the senior prof. He refused the extra load after the Affirmative Action decision was handed down. Later, he refused to come to departmental meetings or to be elected to the Senate. He has shortened his office hours. He says he's not going to take on any extra responsibility. It's all right. It gives us women the chance to finally get elected to the Senate. Bill and his cronies have been pillars of the administration for twenty-five years; it's our turn now."

"And did you hear about the couch?"

"What couch?"

"You didn't hear the details? Carol ordered Bill to remove the big orange couch from his office. She said it looked bad for a professor to have indirect lighting and a couch in his office. Some young girls have complained about his flirting with them when they were on that very couch. He was fuming! He had to have it removed and taken back to his house. It was his personal sofa, not a university property. The floor lamps, too. Carol ordered all sofas removed, which means that Stan, who had one, an old one - he took naps on it before he taught his night class - had to get rid of his couch, also. Poor old Stan, you know what a sports nut he is. He used to park his bicycle behind the couch and change there from his athletic shorts into his corduroys, then he would take a nap before his night class. He's now brought a sleeping bag that he hides in his file cabinet, and he sleeps on the floor on Tuesdays and Thursdays! In a way, it's sad, but funny, too! The interesting thing is, there was not one woman who ever had a couch in her office."

"That's true. And you know there's something else I've noticed. Not one single woman on our floor has an office with a window overlooking the park. We all have inside cubicles with no windows. Something else to investigate one of these days."

"Gosh! I hadn't thought of that, you're right. I wonder if it's that true for the whole building. Anyway, we are supposed to be busy and we've been gossiping here forever. I need to go. Look at the time!"

"*A bientôt*, as we say in frog land."

"Yes, Haaa bientoouu, as you say."

Same Day: 5:30 p.m.

Dean Luponski's secretary smiled at Professor Carol Murray as she ushered her in his office. The dean was expecting the Foreign Languages head. As soon as Carol was in, the secretary returned to her desk and the dean closed the door after her.

"I am so glad you came, Carol. How are your students doing these days?"

"Very well, thank you. They're all working hard, preparing for their midterms. It's a busy time of the year for all of us, as you know. And faculty morale is not good, especially with the budget crunch. I am supposed to turn in next year's budget to you in a week. Dean Luponski, miracles I cannot do. In my department, the entire part-time faculty is on soft money and so are the Graduate Teaching Assistants. I don't see how I can cut back on the number of GTAs or pay them less. You know they are our bread and butter, and not just for us, but for the whole College of Arts and Letters. We bring in the highest number of credits hours in the whole college."

"You don't have to start fighting for your cause, right off the bat. Don't worry, Carol, I'll see what I can do. Turn your budget in with the essentials and we'll look at it carefully and talk again. That's not the reason I called you in. I asked you to come to my office because I had a few questions to pose about one of your colleagues. To come straight to the point, I wanted your opinion about the fellow who was refused tenure at the departmental level."

"Yes, of course, you mean Professor Mayley. It's a sad story."

"I would like you to be candid about this. I'll speak frankly myself. It's so difficult for a dean to get the truth and nothing but the truth. You have the reputation of being direct, sometimes a little too direct for your own good, I might add. Oh, yes, deans have to pay attention to gossip, good and bad, and I hear quite a bit of good about you. The bad is that you shoot yourself in the foot once in a while by being too outspoken, you might say truthful, with some of the faculty in your department."

"I am outspoken, once in a while, and I always regret it, but you know I control my temper and I don't speak out of line in the heat of passion. I have learned to contain myself, at least, some of the time. Even with you! For example, you see, I should have waited for you to speak, instead of rushing right in with my talk about budgets."

"Yes, exactly! Well, I'd like to know what you think of Mayley's teaching. His student evaluations are mediocre. He has not published since he has been here, and that does not endear him to the vice-president. I need to decide soon, since the dean's committee has reiterated that they find no proof of outstanding teaching, publishing, or even service to the University. They, as well as your departmental committee, are recommending a denial of tenure. I need to have ammunition if I am going to fight them, or else I will just take the side of the committees, which is my first instinct, anyway."

"I believe Mayley does an adequate job in the lower-division classes, but he lacks substance and pedagogical savoir-faire in the upper division seminars. The irony is that, though he teaches French, he seems to have little empathy for our French assistants, who are new to this country and lack deep understanding of the American culture. As you may know, they form half of our teaching staff. The lack of sympathy between Mayley and the French graduate students creates unnecessary stress in our department.

"So, the French students criticize him frequently?"

"Yes. In Professor Mayley's defense, you have to understand that French people are used to be critical and love to have discussions. It's in both their make-up and their academic culture. I recognize this in myself too. The French part of my background cannot lie. Perhaps it's because we French love debates so much that we disagree overtly and, sometimes, loudly among ourselves."

"I see…"

"Another source of friction is that Mayley tends to be severe in grading the French GTAs, especially the girls. He corrects wrongly some turns of phrases that are acceptable in French. For example, he may change the French word corresponding to "live" and replace it by "inhabit," a pointless change that illustrates his inability to recognize various levels of discourse in French. Yet he leaves obvious mistakes uncorrected, such as agreement with the past participle. Those French kids know the difference in their native tongue. They laugh at his own mediocre French. It's hard on their morale because they fancy themselves the true essence of Frenchness. They feel an American, even with a Ph.D. should not correct them improperly."

"He's entitled to impose his opinion, I suppose."

He is, on scholarly matters, because of his knowledge of the field, but he does not succeed well at that, either. Tension exists among us, created mostly by him, out of his own insecurity and lack of confidence. He appears tentative and weak, which makes him the laughing stock of the assistants and graduate students, even the American ones."

"Well, you're a true psychologist, Carol, but a pessimist, too. It sounds as if you do not find him a good fit for your department. Do French Graduate students and other colleagues find him lacking in his work on literature?"

"He is mediocre there, too. He is partly alright in his field of poetry. He loves to teach the mechanics of poetry, feet, syllables, how many verses in a sonnet etc., but he has no feel for the poetic content. Still most students agree that his cultural knowledge is inadequate. I must add that his colleagues find his literary scope narrow. And unfortunately, I have to agree."

"How is his spoken French?"

"Euh. . . Not that good..."

"I must say you don't seem too enthusiastic about his spoken language, either."

"I know. I feel bad because I should be able to like him better. He has bought a house here. He has a family, a wife, two sons and I feel sorry for him; but at the same time, we need charismatic, productive people. That's why I signed the denial of tenure though my own department was split about it. On these issues, I am tough. We cannot carry deadwood. People need to carry their weight or the cookie crumbles, the horses run wild, and the sky falls on our heads, if you'll excuse the succession of metaphors!"

"Well, that's that, then. The decision is made. I'll talk to the committee and the vice-president. Be ready to hire a year from now, if we still have the money."

"Don't frighten me, Dean Luponski. Even if we lose him, we have to give him an extra year to look for a job, but please, don't take away the position. In my budget, next week, I am turning in a request for an extra position in French. We need it desperately. So, promise me I can replace Mayley also the following year."

"Come on, Carol, don't use that smile on me. You know I can't make such a promise. We'll see when the time comes."

"All right, but think of my department's plight and, please, keep a little something for us in those pots you have hidden away."

"I wish, I wish... Not many pots left to draw from these days. You should be appealing to your alumni for donations in a more consistent manner, Carol."

"I know, but I don't have the brain of a fundraiser."

"Our administrators keep urging us to tap them as a source of revenue."

"I know..."

"See you soon, Carol, and have a very good day. I mean it. Say hi to Pat and your son Rex for me, won't you?"

5

VILLENEUVE-SUR-LOT, FRANCE
Summer 1980

Julie dashes out the door and down the steps for the third time this morning. The bouquet of gladioli she bought earlier looks stingy. How lucky that today is market day; she can buy fresh flowers and cheese and the special olives she loves. Everything is going to go well this week. She can sense it.

Carol's actually coming. This afternoon, she'll be here. Julie's good fortune began when she learned about this apartment from Lucienne, the secretary at the English School where Julie teaches. Lucienne's sister, Gabrielle, lives here in Villeneuve-sur-Lot and is happy to trade a week in her apartment for a week in Julie's apartment in the city of Agen. It works out well for both of them. Gabrielle and her boyfriend want to spend some time in Agen. And Julie wants a special place for Carol's visit. Agen is pleasant, but since Julie has been living and teaching there for nearly a year, the charm of novelty is gone. Villeneuve is one of the *bastides,* originally fortified cities, with many ancient features that she and Carol can discover together during the week.

Julie thrills at the thought of how soon she'll see Carol and she buys two more clusters of the scarlet gladioli. Hurrying back to the small apartment above the hairdresser's salon, she considers the day's schedule. If Carol is arriving in Agen on the afternoon train from Avignon, Julie should leave Villeneuve at noon in her rented car. It's less than thirty miles to Agen, but Julie doesn't drive much in France, so she'll allow herself some extra time.

The morning sun warms her shoulders through the light cotton blouse as she returns to the apartment with the promise of another hot day. Her forehead creases in a small frown; she worries a little about the heat in the apartment. Will they be sweltering by evening? Still, the freshness of the summer morning is delightful and she realizes she should be enjoying it rather than worrying about possible problems. Giving herself a small shake, Julie vows not to allow the threat of a problem to overshadow the pleasure of the present. Not today. This week she will enjoy every moment as it comes to her.

The chemical cosmetic odors of a busy beauty salon remind Julie that she's reached the apartment and she runs up the stairs, laughing to herself at the American hurry of her ascent. None of her French friends would run up those stairs. In the apartment, she adds the flowers to the ones already in the simple glass vase, the only one she can find. Lucienne's sister has few possessions in her modest home, but, characteristically French, the things she has are well-chosen and attractive. The now generous bouquet glows in the sunny room. Looking around at the sofa, the small round table with two chairs by the open French doors leading out to the tiny balcony, the kitchen area half-hidden by the partition behind the sofa, Julie decides with satisfaction that the room is perfectly charming.

How lovely to have this week with Carol, all to herself. Julie has tried to explain in her letters to Carol how important she is to Julie. How much she loves her. Nearly seven years ago, when Julie first transferred to Meriwether University from Oregon State University and found herself in Carol's Survey of French Literature class, this, she believes, was when her intellectual life, her adult life began. Her life of the mind, life of the heart.

After one year of college, the small-town atmosphere at Corvallis had felt restrictive and Julie arranged to move to Portland and transfer to Meriwether University. The Portland setting seemed vastly more cosmopolitan to the nineteen-year old and she delighted in the independence of her own tiny apartment, made possible by her part-time job in the university library and a small bequest from her paternal grandfather willing to help his only grandchild move into a wider world.

When Julie declared French as her major in the fall of 1974, and Carol Murray became her adviser, Julie was thrilled. Her classes with the witty and charismatic professor had already persuaded her that Carol was her ideal woman. Carol's intelligence, sophistication and kindness to her students made her an excellent adviser. As she guided Julie through her academic career and two years of teaching high school French, their relationship had deepened, becoming friends and confidantes.

Last year, when Julie decided to take the risk of moving to France, Carol had been the one consistently encouraging voice. Julie knows that without Carol's support, she would never have had the courage to leave her job and to find her current teaching position in Agen.

Julie thinks of her past year of teaching and smiles ruefully. She likes living in France, and is delighted that her French is now fluent, but it was surprising how quickly the glamour wore off her new living situation. She learned that a cold winter apartment is as bleak in Agen as it is in Portland. The disdain of an unfriendly store clerk chiding you for being in the wrong line is no more pleasant because it's expressed in French. Being short of francs at the end of the month is in no way superior to being short of dollars. But Julie has survived a low period in late November and another in late January, when the Dordogne seemed to have lost the sun forever. Since the return of blue skies in the springtime, she has once again been able to take pleasure in her French sojourn.

She still debates with herself whether she will stay in Agen another year, and she looks forward to being able to discuss the decision with Carol in the coming week. Julie's usually serious face is lit by a smile at the prospect of a whole week in which to share long, intimate talks with Carol.

The morning is nearly gone and Julie remembers that she has not made a dinner reservation at *La Fontaine*, one of the nicest restaurants in town where she wants to take Carol for their first dinner together.

Running back down the stairs, Julie sees the two hairdressers exchange comments and laugh. She reaches La Fontaine and calms herself to speak with the restaurant proprietor in the cool, serious manner she has found most successful, recalling Carol's warning that most Americans smile too much in France giving an impression of insincerity and over-familiarity. She remembers Carol's demonstration of the proper demeanor: slight frown, lips pursed, a cool and brief, "*deux pour dîner, s'il vous plaît.*" No garrulous explanation offered by so many tourists trying to be friendly. Julie understands by this time that friendliness is not considered a necessary component of business transactions in France. When Julie has established that *deux pour dîner à huit heures* will be no problem, she leaves her name and returns to the apartment to dress for her trip to Agen.

What to wear? It's important to look exactly right when she meets Carol: more sophisticated than her Portland self, but not over-dressed for a train platform on a summer day. After some deliberation, Julie decides on a short blue linen skirt and a fresh white silk shirt. Instead of a scarf, which she discards as too fussy, she adds a chunky necklace of bright blue donkey beads that she picked up in the local market.

Handbag and car keys in hand, Julie descends the stairs at a sedate pace which escapes the notice of the hairdressers. Retrieving the rental car from the pleasant g*aragiste*, Julie maneuvers cautiously out of town and on to the N.21, direction Agen. There is more traffic than she expected, much more than when she drove north yesterday evening. She finds that if she stays in the right-hand lane and keeps her speed at 80 km per hour, except when crossing villages, she moves along fine and the big Peugeot sedans can pass her as they wish.

Happily, the school where Julie teaches is only a few blocks from the Agen train station, so she finds parking with no difficulty. She parks the little Renault, locks it, and deposits a few francs in the parking meter on the corner. Glancing at her watch, she sees that there's time to walk to the shops in the center of town and visit a favorite bookstore where she picks up the new Marguerite Duras novel as a welcoming gift for Carol.

Julie makes her purchase quickly, hoping Carol has not read it yet, and returns to the station.

The train from Avignon arrives promptly, and Julie realizes she's holding her breath as passengers pour onto the platform. The August holidays mean full trains, and the platform is quickly packed with travelers. Clutching the newly-purchased book and her handbag, Julie dives eagerly into the crowd and moves closer to the train, scanning the crowd for a familiar form. Her gaze passes over an older woman, short, a little stooped, bouffant blonde wig slightly askew, who is struggling with a large handbag and a heavy suitcase unwieldy on inadequate wheels.

There is something familiar that calls her attention back just as the woman turns. It's Carol. Oh, she's getting old, crosses Julie's mind. She loyally brushes it away and moves quickly toward Carol, touching her arm. Carol looks up and her tense expression relaxes into the wide affectionate smile Julie loves.

"Carol, you're here! At last!"

"Julie, *chérie*. I'm so glad to be here."

They greet each other with an American hug, then laugh and exchange *bises* in proper French fashion.

"Ah, Julie, it's wonderful to see you. You look lovely. Very chic. I love the necklace."

Julie laughs, feeling young and slightly shy. She gives the book to Carol who is delighted at the thoughtfulness of the gift. She has not read it. As Julie guides her toward the street the older woman tells of her recent travels.

"The trip to Avignon, two days ago, was easy on the express train. But, today's trip, *mon Dieu*! There were no seats available on the morning express, so I had to take the slower train and the air conditioning seemed to have broken down. I feel as though I've been on that train for days. My head is splitting; my ankles are swollen."

"Ah, but you're here now. Here's the car. Good, your suitcase fits in the trunk perfectly and we can get on the road right away. Oh, but I should have asked. Do you need a rest stop?"

"No, I'm fine. The lavatories on the train were perfectly adequate. Actually, before I get into another vehicle why don't we have a Calvados at that café across the street? Is your parking time OK?"

"Sure. I'll put a little more change in the meter. Yes, by all means, let's have a drink there. It will relax you. It's early yet. There's no need to hurry."

Carol settles into the chair at the café with a sigh and rummages in her purse for her pill box. Her head is throbbing. Really, after that exhausting train ride, perhaps one more Valium would do no harm. It's been several hours since she took the last one. And there is still the drive north to Villeneuve-sur-Lot. When the waiter comes, she orders their drinks and a *pichet* of water to take her pill."

Carol looks up at Julie's eager face as she returns from the parking area and smiles gently. It is good to be in company of such youth and freshness again.

"By the way, Julie, in Avignon I ran into my old friends from Portland, the Warrens, Liz and Morris. They have rented a car and are touring across the South of France from Avignon to Bordeaux, so I suggested that they meet us for dinner in Villeneuve-sur-Lot tomorrow evening."

She notices Julie's silence and, taking it for shyness, she adds reassuringly. "I think you met them at Meriwether, didn't you? Morris Warren, from the history department, just retired last year when I did. You'll like them, I know. Liz is so gracious and Morris has a wonderful sense of humor."

"Of course, I remember taking his History of Modern Europe course. And I met Mrs. Warren at your house, remember? Two Christmases ago. It will be nice to see them again."

"While I think about it, Fanny Taylor, from the French department at Meriwether, I know you had some classes with her your senior year, is spending the summer with her mother not far from Villeneuve; a village with a funny name: beouffton? Ton boeff? No, Tombeboeuf. It translates in Fall-bull? I wonder what circumstances could have given the village its name." Carol chuckles, taking another sip of her Calvados.

"Anyway, I called Fanny when I was in Paris and when she heard I was going to be in Villeneuve-sur-Lot, she insisted that we join her family for a real French picnic. Doesn't that sound fabulous? I thought we could do that on Monday. It seemed to be a good date for Fanny and her household."

At the look on Julie's face, now distinctly downcast, Carol smiles coaxingly over her drink. "Come, dear Julie, tell me you're not angry. I know, Pat would scold me for doing so much arranging of things, but we have many days together. It's only Friday and I'm here with you until Tuesday afternoon."

"Tuesday?" Julie gasps, "I thought you could stay until Thursday. I have…"

"Oh, I am sorry. Is that a misunderstanding? I was sure I told you Tuesday when we spoke on the telephone. I have to be back in Paris on Wednesday. Oh Julie, I'll feel terrible if I've inconvenienced you."

"No, no, of course not. It's not an inconvenience. It's just, yes, just a disappointment. The time we have together is so precious to me, that's all."

"I know, dear. It's precious to me, too. And we have these lovely four days together. That's a lot really. Right?" Carol smiles placating her friend.

Swallowing her disappointment, Julie returns the smile and empties her glass of chilled grapefruit juice. Carol finishes the last of her Calvados, and they set off for the car. By this time, Friday afternoon rush hour has joined the heavy holiday traffic and Julie's attention is absorbed by the effort to negotiate their trip to Villeneuve-sur-Lot without incident. Carol, having learned to drive rather recently herself, knows better than to distract Julie and allows herself to float peacefully on waves of Valium, Calvados and fatigue on the way to Villeneuve.

On reaching the apartment, Carol is touched to see Julie's preparations for her arrival: the lovely bouquet, a bottle of Sancerre chilling in the refrigerator, some fresh *chèvre* cheese with herbs. The two women spend a pleasant hour on the small balcony, catching up on news of mutual friends and watching the glow of the descending sun on the ancient town towers as the people in the street below return home.

"Villeneuve-sur-Lot," Carol muses. "Funny. Villeneuve was the name of one of my professors at the University of Chicago back in the '40s. He was a 'right bastard' as my Irish friends would say. To think that he shares a name with this lovely place."

Carol and Julie exchange family news.

"Pat and Rex. How are things going for them?"

Carol, growing serious, tells of Pat's increasing respiratory problems. "For so many years we've known that his kidneys could fail him at any time. It seems terribly unfair that he has to fight these problems with his lungs. He's been so courageous for so long. Recently I feel as though he's, well, I don't want to say giving up, maybe it's more that he's losing some of his old resilience. Really, how many times can I ask him to pick himself back up again? We celebrated our thirty-seventh anniversary the week before I came on this trip. I realized that he has been fighting these extreme health problems our entire married life."

"What a hard thing for him, for you, and Rex."

"Well, it's just been part of our lives and we've got through it as best we could, crisis by crisis."

"And you've remained amazing human beings through it all."

Carol chuckles softly, "I don't know about amazing, but," then serious this time, "in the last few months Pat has been very depressed. You know five or six years ago, when you first knew us, he was studying the stock market with great discipline and he got very good results for our little nest egg. It was such a good thing for him because it's always been hard for him that I have had to be the family breadwinner over the years. Now that he's not well enough anymore to guide our investments, he's feeling depressed. I think it's affecting his physical health."

"So, he has failed in this past year, physically, and in the stock market, too?"

"Oh yes. You'll notice a real difference when you see him. He still has those rare wonderful moments. He sent his love to you and made me promise that we'd drink a bottle of Bergerac just for him."

"Dear Pat. And how is Rex? You said he's begun a course to become an optician?"

"Yes. Did I write you that the man who gave him the initial examination said Rex had the highest level of digital dexterity he had ever measured? He seems to be doing all right in the courses. I'm not sure whether this will work out or not. It's sometimes hard for me to imagine Rex actually in a job where he would have to be there each day, have to deal with strangers. . . I don't know."

Suddenly, Carol looks old and weary.

"I wonder. You know these before-dinner snacks have been so delightful. We really don't need to go out to dinner, do we? We could just. . ." She stops, seeing Julie's crestfallen face, and says firmly, "No, no. You have made arrangements. Of course, we'll go out to dinner. I'm fine."

"But Carol, if you don't feel up to it?"

"Not at all. I'm up to it. I just felt tired for a moment there. I want to take advantage of every moment of this trip. Who knows when I will be in France again?"

Carol picks up her cosmetic bag and goes into the bathroom. Emerging ten minutes later, freshly made up, with the perky blonde wig properly in place, she says brightly, "Now then, I'll put on my restaurant dress, shall I? I have a dining out dress and a dining out blouse and skirt. Tonight, the dress gets the nod."

"I'll just comb my hair." Julie says, slipping into the tiny bathroom.

At *La Fontaine*, Julie can see that Carol is making an effort throughout dinner to carry her share of the conversation but several times she lapses into silence, clearly enjoying the excellent food, the savor of the canard confit, the mellow wine, the velvet *crème brûlée*. Julie, with her American habit of combining food and continual conversation at times feels she is conducting a monologue.

Though she knows Carol is doing the best she can, by the end of the evening, Julie feels vaguely disappointed in the way the evening has gone. Carol is obviously content with the lovely dinner, however, and too weary to begin a discussion in the late evening. Carol will need a good night's sleep to be ready for the next day's sightseeing, so Julie gives her a glass of water for her sleeping pills and sees her sink gratefully into Gabrielle's bed.

The sun of another lovely August morning slips between the aging shutters, making a pattern on the ceiling. The light wakens Julie, curled on the small living room couch. She has slept fitfully and opens her eyes with a slightly apprehensive feeling. Oh, Carol's friends, the Warrens, are coming later today. Peering fuzzily at the clock, she realizes she'd better hurry to the boulangerie or the tourists will have taken the entire morning's supply of fresh croissants.

Carol sleeps heavily until after 10:30 when the telephone wakes her. She lifts her head and Julie sees her rub her forehead and close her eyes for a few minutes while Julie makes arrangements to meet the Warrens for dinner at a restaurant overlooking the River Lot. Gathering her toilet articles, Carol slips into the bathroom, giving Julie a quick wave on the way.

"Oh, that coffee smells heavenly." Carol gives Julie a little hug and joins her at the breakfast table, prettily set with Gabrielle's gay Provencal pottery and laden with *café au lait*, croissants, and *confiture de fraises*, Carol's favorite French strawberry jam.

"The Warrens want us to join them at their hotel for drinks before dinner and I wasn't sure what to say, so I said that should be fine."

"Oh, of course, why not? Morris Warren always travels with the best Scotch. This is a lovely breakfast, Julie. Thank you. I slept longer than I expected."

"I'm sure you were tired from your traveling yesterday."

"I suppose." Grimacing slightly, "I think it's a mistake to dwell on the deterioration of the body brought on by age, but I must say, I miss the energy I had twenty years ago," Carol says with a rueful laugh. "And these headaches are a nuisance. Do you have a little water? I'll take this medication the doctor gave me. It's strong and it usually works fairly quickly."

Julie brings the water and asks, "What would you like to do today?"

"Well, what is particularly recommended for visiting in Villeneuve-sur-Lot, Mademoiselle?" Carol asks with a fond half-smile.

After a brief discussion, they decide to explore the Roman-Byzantine Sainte Catherine's church in the morning and visit the Musée Gaston Rapin after lunch.

After a good morning of sightseeing, laughter, and shared memories, they enjoy a late lunch at a café and then Carol confesses that her headache has returned. Julie suggests they return to the apartment so that Carol can relax and rest during the heat of the afternoon.

At seven in the evening, they set off to meet Mr. and Mrs. Warren at their hotel. Mrs. Warren is waiting for them in the lobby. Carol greets her affectionately and introduces Julie, who's standing off to one side. Later Julie reflects that that is how she feels the entire evening: slightly off to one side. The Warrens and Carol have three stiff drinks each before they leave for the restaurant. By this time, Dr. Warren is revealing a ribald sense of humor which Carol seems to find hilarious. Julie realizes with some irritation that it's difficult to be the one sober member of a tipsy party. The Warrens insist on treating Carol and Julie to dinner and the man supervises everything, beginning by seating Carol on his right and Julie on his left.

When Carol and Julie return to the apartment after dinner, Julie is tightlipped and silent. Carol, concern for Julie overcoming her high spirits from earlier in the evening, asks, "Is everything all right, Julie?"

"It is. No, no. Everything is not alright. We've just spent an interminable evening with an old lecher who fondled my knee all through dessert."

"Oh, dear. That old rascal. Was he fondling your knee, too? Oh, you mustn't take Morris seriously, dear. He just likes women. I imagine he's led Liz a merry chase over the years."

"And all those self-serving stories about how heroic he was in the days when you were working so hard for affirmative action!"

"Well, he was a real ally and we were truly grateful to the male colleagues who were willing to speak out for our cause.

I'm sorry, dear. I'm sure it's a bore for a pretty young girl to spend an evening with three old cronies and their war stories."

"It's not that. It's just that I think Mr. Warren is a repulsive old goat and we wasted one of our whole evenings with him and his milk-toast wife." To her chagrin, Julie feels her eyes fill with tears.

Carol, observant even through a veil of alcohol and fatigue, notices and comes over to Julie. She puts her arms around Julie and hugs her.

"Oh, Julie, Julie, don't be too hard on us old folks." As she starts to kiss Julie on the cheek, Julie turns her head and their lips meet.

Carol, startled, draws back, and chuckles softly, "Well, that was a French moment, wasn't it? Good night, dear. Get a good night's sleep. Morris Warren will seem less monstrous in the morning."

The next day Carol is feeling unwell and sleeps through most of the morning. She suggests a roast chicken dinner at a nearby brasserie in the early afternoon and then rests again until evening. Julie, disappointed and lonely, visits the municipal museum that she and Carol had planned to visit the previous afternoon.

By evening, Carol is sufficiently recovered to suggest a walk down by the river and back up through the higher section of town to the *Porte de Paris*, one of the remaining towers of the ancient town wall. They stop for part of a Vespers service at Sainte Catherine Church and then stroll back to the apartment, chatting lightly of memories and travel adventures. The intimacy Julie had hoped to feel seems to be missing. Carol is warm and talkative, but a little distant. They agree that an early night is sensible since Monday will be a busy day.

Julie and Carol are to meet Fanny at her mother's summer home in Tombeboeuf at eleven in the morning, so after their breakfast they spend a little time in the local shops.

Carol laughs, "To quote my Chicago friend Mary Maloney, we can't just go empty-handed with our arms hangin' down!" But they know, too, that Mme. Gautier will have a picnic prepared for them, so they decide on a bottle of wine and a box of Swiss chocolates from the local *confiserie*.

The road from Villeneuve to Tombeboeuf is about twenty miles over the kind of country roads Julie most enjoys driving. The morning is beautiful, bright, fresh and scented with summer, and even Julie's mood lifts at the prospect of the day's outing.

Carol has directions from Fanny: through the village, past the church two streets, left up a hill—the house will be on the right, a small sign on the front gate, *Beaulieu.* Ah, there it is. Fanny stands under an acacia in the front yard with her small son playing at her feet.

Fanny sees the car arrive and moves quickly to greet them. Julie is struck with a pang of jealousy as she sees the beautiful young mother, so poised, so French, greet her friend and colleague from America.

Fanny turns immediately to include Julie in her welcome and thanks her for bringing Carol. "This is lovely. How nice that you're so nearby, Julie. Here, you must meet my son, Jeff. Jeff, *chéri, viens ici.* He has spent all summer speaking French, so he may resist going back to English." She laughs.

Jeff says his *Bonjour* dutifully with a shy smile, then runs back to his trucks among the trees of the garden where he has constructed a network of roads for the city of his imagination.

"What a lovely spot!" Carol exclaims looking around. She laughs when she spies a small patch of bamboo in a corner of the garden. "You see! It is perfect! Even bamboo. Pat always says no garden could be perfect without some bamboo."

A handsome woman about Carol's age has just emerged from the house. "Carol," Fanny says, putting her arm around the older woman, "You remember my mother, Céleste. I believe you met when she visited us in Portland."

"*Bien sûr, Mme. Gautier! Enchantée de vous revoir.*" They greet each other with warmth. Introductions are made and Julie is drawn into the welcoming circle of their friendship.

"Mother has things nearly organized for the picnic. We'll take her car and that way we'll have enough room for all our picnic paraphernalia, and for Jeff and his toy trucks!" She turns to Carol, "I thought, we would just drive through some of the local wine country; it's so lovely this time of year. We'll stop whenever we find a likely spot or when we're hungry!"

"That sounds heavenly!"

Soon, the expedition is underway, everyone in high spirits and chatting rapidly, at times simultaneously, in French. Although kind attempts are made to include Julie in the conversation, Fanny, Carol, and Céleste are soon launched on a cheerful argument, brought on by Carol's mention of the novel Julie has given her, as to which modern writers from the South of France have real lasting value and which will turn out to have been passing fancies of the literary world. Julie finds herself with little to contribute and spends most of the time watching the passing scenery through the car window.

About one o'clock, just as Jeff is beginning to complain about being hungry, Fanny sees a lovely hillside vineyard with trees separating it from a small stream. It is a lovely spot for a picnic and she eases the car down a lane running along the margin of the vineyard and turns off the engine.

"Everybody out," she says cheerfully. "Lunchtime!" The party unceremoniously piles out of the car. Soon, they have spread Céleste's picnic on the grassy verge of the lane a short distance from the car. On a bright cotton cloth, they set out four kinds of olives, a rich pate, cornichons, a pottery bowl filled with fresh greens, baguettes and a round loaf of rustic bread, a plate of sliced summer ripe tomatoes with herbs, radishes and butter, three kinds of cheese and the bottle of wine, Carol and Julie's offering. Under a napkin to the side an apricot tart and several plump peaches are waiting. Céleste has seen to arrangements down to the smallest details. There are proper glasses for the wine, carefully packed in colorful print napkins; there are knives to cut the bread, nothing has been forgotten.

The four women and the little boy launch into their meal with sharp appetites stimulated by fresh air, lovely surroundings, and good company. As they eat, their conversation slows and becomes lighter than in the car as they give attention to the food. Céleste, always the generous hostess, keeps an eye on her guests, supplying bread for the pâté and butter for the radishes, and making sure the wine glasses are replenished.

Young Jeff finishes his *Orangina* drink and begins to drive his trucks in and out among the vines at the edge of the vineyard. Julie sees Carol look over at Fanny and exchange a look of perfect contentment. Carol sighs and murmurs, "La Belle France!"

Carol, Céleste, and Fanny all lean back happily and Julie sees that they are beginning to doze lightly. Julie sits beside Jeff and his trucks a while and then, with the restlessness of the young, gets to her feet and moves toward the brook half hidden below the trees. She walks for ten or fifteen minutes, strolling along the grassy bank, catching glimpses of the bright summer clothing of the picnic group beyond the trees.

As she begins to turn back, she hears Fanny calling, "Jeff... Jeffie, Julie, Julie."

Julie starts to back up on the small slope and works her way among the trees and thin undergrowth, emerging at last near the open area of their picnic ground.

"Ah, Julie!" Fanny cries with relief, when Julie is still at some distance, "Jeff is with you?"

"No, no." Julie stammers.

"He was playing with his trucks there by the vines. I just took a walk down by the stream.

The older women look at each other in alarm, and Fanny, who is already standing, runs over to Jeff's trucks. She looks up the vine rows, calling more urgently, "Jeff, Jeff!"

Carol asks worriedly, "Did Jeff follow you toward the stream, Julie?"

"No. I mean, I don't think he did. He seemed so absorbed in his play. I thought he'd stay by his mother."

"I shouldn't have taken my eyes off him," Fanny wails.

Céleste's soothing voice says, "We'll find him soon. He'll be fine. He cannot have gone far in this length of time."

Céleste suggests that Carol and Fanny climb the vine-covered hill above the spot where Jeff had been playing. Then if Julie will retrace her path to be sure Jeff didn't follow her down by the stream, Céleste herself will wait by the car and sound the horn intermittently in case Jeff finds his own way back.

Carol and Fanny hurry up the hill, calling Jeff's name. Julie returns to the half-overgrown path she had taken earlier. She senses that she has been irresponsible, unintentionally certainly, but irresponsible nonetheless. She hears behind her the calls of Carol and Fanny carried on the summer air and the intermittent honk of the car horn.

Julie notices that the atmosphere has become sultrier and looking up she sees that dark clouds are massing in the western sky. The darkness seems ominous and she suppresses a shudder. For the next five minutes, Julie hears the voices grow farther away as Carol and Fanny reach the top of the hill and then closer again as they start back down. It is a long, sad time for Julie, who feels alternately guilty, defensive and frightened that the little boy might actually have followed her down to the creek where she now sees there are pools that could be dangerous for a child.

Julie hears two happy calls from midway down the hillside. "Here he is! *On l'a trouvé!*" Her knees trembling with relief, she sits on a fallen log a moment to collect herself. Rejoining Céleste at their picnic spot, Julie can see the smile on Fanny's face as she reaches the bottom of the hill with her dusty boy.

"Ah. *Grâce à Dieu!*" Céleste cries taking her grandson from his mother's arms.

"He had been playing under the vines halfway up the hill with his red truck," Fanny laughs, full of joy at the safe reappearance of her son. They gather around the six-year-old, chattering their relief.

"And while we catch our breaths, some apricot tart?"

"Mother, is there coffee in the thermos?"

Quickly the women set out the fragrant pastry and busy themselves serving it. The dessert seems all the more exquisite for their awareness of escape from tragedy and the laughter and exclamations of the three older women restore the party nearly to its previous mood. But Julie cannot shake off the somber feelings of the worry and the search. Life seems suddenly precarious and happiness unspeakably fragile. She is almost relieved when, just as they are finishing the last of the tart, fat drops of rain begin to fall from the gathered clouds in the darkening sky bringing the picnic to an end.

"Quickly, quickly," Fanny laughs. "Gather it all up. Whoops, Jeffie, into the car! Carol, are you alright? Julie, do you have that cloth, please? Into the car everybody! Voilà." Laughing and scrambling, they load the picnic articles and climb into the car.

Just as they close the car doors, the heavens open and Fanny cautiously backs out of the lane onto the country road, peering through the downpour.

"Now! Weren't we lucky? The weather lasted just long enough for our afternoon tea. How convenient."

The drive back to Tombeboeuf is a quiet one with Jeff nestled in his grandmother's arms and Fanny concentrating on driving through the rainstorm. Julie rests her head against the back of the seat, closes her eyes, attempting to overcome the sense of isolation that has been building throughout the day.

Back at Céleste's *Beaulieu*, the party, tired from the exertions of the day, unloads the car. Fortunately, the summer showers have moved off to the north of Tombeboeuf and they don't have to contend with rain or mud, but the sky looks threatening. Fanny and Céleste agree that the two other women should make their return trip to Villeneuve while the weather holds. Céleste presses on them a small packet with leftover pâté and cheese and the rosy peaches. Farewells are said, thanks given. Fanny and Carol can say *au revoir* until they meet again back in Portland in the fall. Both Céleste and Fanny say a warmly polite goodbye to Julie and she responds, but finds herself wondering whether an apology is owed. Was it her fault about Jeff? But she prefers to think not and the moment passes. She thanks Fanny and Céleste for their hospitality and the memorable day and slides into the driver's seat of her little rented Renault.

Julie and Carol talk very little on the return trip to Villeneuve-sur-Lot. By this time, Carol seems exhausted from the day's outing and she sleeps most of the way back to Gabrielle's apartment. When they arrive, Julie suggests dinner out, but Carol insists that she has eaten too much through the day. Just a small snack from Mme. Gautier's parcel, and then she will be ready to retire with her novel.

"I'm sorry, dear," she smiles ruefully. "I know I'm not very lively company. It was a wonderful day, but it was tiring. With tomorrow's trip, I must get a good rest tonight."

After Carol is settled for the evening, Julie sits on the balcony sipping a glass of wine, thinking how far short of her expectations Carol's visit has fallen. She remembers the dark winter months when one of her chief delights was writing long, chatty letters to Carol. Carol always responded warmly, though her letters were neither as frequent nor as lengthy as Julie's. Julie recalls the picture of Carol she keeps on the piano in her apartment in Agen so that when she's playing, it's as though she's playing for Carol. She's almost hypnotized by those deep set, melancholy eyes that seem to return her gaze.

So, when Carol was going to come and to stay with her for a whole week, Julie was sure their relationship would move to a new deeper level of intimacy, a meeting of souls. But that hasn't happened. In fact, Julie realizes that much of her depression today stems from the fact that Carol seemed closer to and fonder of Fanny than of herself, Julie. She winces at the adolescent envy she feels, but the sorrow in her heart remains.

The next day, Carol rises late and by the time they have breakfasted and she has packed her bags, it is time to drive to Agen. The midday traffic is not bad on this Tuesday, and they arrive in time for a stroll around Agen and lunch at a shady sidewalk café. The heaviness of the air from yesterday was not broken by showers in this area, and the oppressive weather seems to match the women's mood.

They chat superficially about Agen, about what Carol will see and about her return to Paris.

After a brief silence, Carol, sensing Julie's low spirits, turns to her and says gently, "Thank you, Julie dear. Thank you for all this visit has been, the sweet apartment, the lovely dinner on Saturday, the beautiful French breakfasts. You have given me so much."

As Julie starts to brush off her thanks, Carol continues, "I feel, Julie, that this visit has disappointed you in some way. But

I just want you to know that, for me, it has been a perfect time. I hope that you will not dwell on what the time was not but that you will remember with pleasure what it was. I thank you for the beautiful memories I am taking home from this visit."

"You haven't disappointed me. It isn't that. It's just, it's just that I *love* you." Julie cries. "I know, dear. And I love you, too." Carol stands, ready to meet her train; she leans over, gives Julie's shoulders a squeeze and kisses her on the top of her lowered head.

After the train departed and she has waved a last farewell to Carol, Julie returns to her parked car, leans her head on her arms, and sobs.

6

CHICAGO
Spring 1949

"Hello?"

"Hello, this is Tony. May I speak to Mary Maloney?" Tony said in a formal tone, but he had already recognized Mary's voice.

"Well, hi, Tony. Yes, it's Mary. Good heavens, a voice from the past. Are you in Chicago?"

The two old college friends were happy to recognize each other's voices after their years of university together. A voice was a distinctive as fingerprints, Mary thought. Both were also friends of Judith Carol Murray and, immediately the image of Carol entered Mary's mind.

"Yeah, I'm calling from my mother's. She had to go out this evening. I've been here for a few days visiting Mom and doing some research. I'm glad I reached you. I wasn't sure you'd be at the old number. It's a while since I've talked to you."

"Yes, it must be over two years, the summer before you moved to Boston. In fact, didn't I see you at that going-away party at Elizabeth's? Anyway, I'm still here in my same apartment. Aren't you glad to know some things stay the same? How are things on the East Coast? How's Lucy?"

"Oh, we're fine, thanks. Is the Maloney clan still running Chicago, all those Irish aunts and uncles and dozens of cousins?"

"Ah, shure, we're flourishin' and multiplyin'! I think the Maloneys may be in large part responsible for this Baby Boom they're talking about! It's a good thing I'm upholding the ranks of maiden aunthood. Are you and Lucy contributing to the growth of America yet?"

"Not yet. We're hoping to get into a house by summer, then we can start thinking about the patter of little feet. But I wanted to tell you. I ran into Judith this afternoon at the Art Institute, I'd sneaked off to have a look at the Ansel Adams exhibit. Judith's looking great, have you seen her lately?"

"Ah, Judith-also-known-as-Carol Murray?"

"Hey, what was it with that name change? I never heard why we went from Judith to Carol."

"Oh, didn't you ever hear that story? The way she tells it is that when she met Pat and they got engaged, he told her he really didn't like the name Judith and he thought Pat and Judy sounded like a cheap nightclub act, so she decided to use her middle name, Carol. She said she'd read that it's a Chinese custom to change your name for a new phase of your life and the idea pleased her. She decided her new name for married life would be Carol."

"So, that's it. Well, I think she'll always be Judith to me."

"Yeah, most of her old school-friends still call her Judith and she doesn't seem to mind. Anyway, in answer to your first question, I haven't seen her for a couple of months. Not since New Year's, I guess. How is she?"

"Great. She was telling me about her new job teaching at Loyola College. I thought she was still at that girls' school where she was teaching when she got married."

"Phillips? She was there a couple of years, but they had an opening at Loyola and Judith was glad to move to higher Ed. She'd always wanted to teach college level, I think. She likes not having so many extra activities and being in a more intellectual atmosphere. You know Judith, for all her kidding around, she has that sharp brain and she likes to use it."

"That's true, she is smart."

"She enjoyed her time at Phillips, too. She's really good at making the best of a situation. Do you remember her first teaching job in that little town in Iowa? I still remember a funny letter she wrote me about going to all the auctions of farm animals and loving to watch pigs. I mean a city girl who can find pigs fascinating, is a pretty adaptable creature!"

"That's for sure. How about you, Mary? Speaking of adaptable creatures, are you still with Chicago Public Schools?"

"Oh, yes, still the dedicated public servant. I'm working on my administrative credential, too. It looks like public schools are one place a woman is going to have a chance of moving up and getting a little power. Even with all the men coming back after the war, we still have them outnumbered in public school positions, so the higher ups have no choice but to advance some of us. But, listen, Tony, did Carol say how Pat's doing?"

"I asked and she said he's doing pretty well. Then she said, 'for now at least' and changed the subject. What is Pat's physical problem, anyway? It always seemed a bit mysterious."

"It's some kind of chronic kidney thing. Pretty serious, I guess. It started when he was in the army, but I've never been clear on whether his work in the service caused it or whether it's just more of a congenital thing. I remember something Judith said one time. It sounded like he might have been involved in Army Intelligence, MIS, FBI or something like that. That might have something to do with the problems he has now. When I tried to follow up on it, she changed the subject, though. But I know he has these terribly painful bouts. They can come on suddenly and last for weeks at a time."

"Jeez. Army Intelligence? Probably. That's a rough thing to have to live with. So, what's he doing? I mean professionally. I didn't want to ask Judith too many questions."

"I think Pat's still taking some courses and trying to be a cartoonist. He draws very well. A field like that is hard to break into, and when we talked at the New Year's Eve party, he sounded discouraged. It's hard because sometimes he'll suddenly have to go into the VA hospital. And he never knows how long he'll be there; so, he can't hold down much of a job. At this stage, he just kind of picks up odd jobs, I guess. It must be hard for a big good-looking man like Pat with first-rate brains and so much charm not to be able to get into a real profession."

"Yeah. That's a devil of a thing. I hadn't realized his health problems were so serious. I mean how can they plan on anything? It has to be a real disruption in their lives. But Judith seems happy. She said they just bought a house."

"Oh, yes, a cute little place over on Laurel St., not too far from her mom and aunt's place. She and Pat had a great New Year's Eve party there. A lot of the old gang, lots of good music and plenty of beer. Joe Brandt was there. Have you seen Joe lately? Weren't you the one who told me that he had a hard time during the war?"

"Yeah, he got into some tough action over in Europe."

"Well, I guess the last few years he's been living in France, trying to get some exchange programs set up for the Illinois University system but he's back in Chicago now."

"Yeah, I guess the last time I heard from him was a couple of years ago, a Christmas card from France. How's he doing?"

"He looks good. He's taken some administrative position with the University system here in Chicago. He's quite the cosmopolitan after his time in France, but he's still a friendly old guy."

"I always thought he and Judith might end up getting married."

"Yeah, she really liked Joe, I know, when we were all in college together. She liked you too, actually! Weren't you smitten with her also? But it was nothing like when she met Pat in '43. Pat and Judith were just the classic case of a love-at-first-sight war-time romance."

"I have to admit it seems to have worked out well."

"You can see they're happy together. Just little things, the way they'll look at each other. They have the same sense of humor and when you spend an evening with them you spend most of it laughing."

"Well, marriage sure seems to have agreed with Judith. She looks great. She was all dolled up at the Art Institute. She had this cute little hat on and a bright scarf around her neck that looked just right. There was always something stylish about the way she dressed. When she speaks French, I always think she sure looks the part. Oh, yeah, I asked her about her Mom and she says she's doing OK."

"Oh, yes. Martha and Aunt Minnie are muddling along fine, enjoying ill health pretty much as they always have. You knew Judith's dad died a couple of years ago, didn't you? Poor old guy."

"Yeah. I'd heard that. He must have been quite an age."

"About 84 or 85, I think. He was a lot older than Judith's mother. He was over 50 when Judith was born. He hadn't been well for a while and, God be good to him, it must have been quite a relief to trade Martha and Minnie in for St. Peter. Martha could be awfully sharp with the poor old soul. I heard Pat ask Judith once why her mom was so mean to poor old Henry!"

"Now was he French? I know he spoke with a bit of an accent."

"Yeah, but he wasn't French. He was Danish, born in Copenhagen."

"Well, where did the French in Judith's family come from?"

"I'm not positive; I think her grandmother on her mother's side was from France. Judith's mom was born in Minnesota, I know that much, and her grandfather on her mom's side was German, but the grandmother was French."

"Yes, Judith really did grow up speaking French, I think, even if her mom was born in Minnesota. I was never sure. Do you know?"

"No. But she spent one whole year in Minnesota when we were in college. Helping a sick aunt, I think. For all I know they may have been speaking French!"

"I know her French is first-rate and I always just assumed it was her first language. She does have a real knack for languages. I mean she's hardly studied any Italian, but I've seen her get along just fine with the waiters at that little Italian place down by the Art Institute."

"Yeah, she is good at languages. She was the star pupil in Sr. Mary Margaret's language classes back in our Mercy High School days."

"That's right. I keep forgetting that you guys have known each other since high school."

"Oh, my yes. We got to be good friends when she saved me from failing French our junior year and disgracing the Maloney family name. I still remember when we met you at St. Teresa College, in that Spanish class I had to suffer through to get my B.A. Remember that?"

"Sure, I remember. Judith and I were together in the Master's Program at the University. Jeez. You wanna talk suffering. You don't know the meaning of the word until you've lived through one of old Villeneuve's seminars."

"Oh, I remember Judith weepin' and wailin' about those times. You know she and I were talking one time and she told me that she thought all foreign language professionals were kind of neurotic."

"Well, thanks a lot!"

"Oh, I'm sure you and she are the exceptions that prove her rule."

"But, I mean, why should foreign language people be any more neurotic than anyone else?"

"Well, Judith's theory was that a lot of them are trying to escape themselves. They're trying to find a new way of being that suits them better than their native situation, because they're never quite happy with who they are."

"Hmm. I have to admit that I can certainly think of some examples that fit her theory! But for a lot of us it's not as much escaping as it is following up some personal interest or family background, like Judith with her French and me with my Italian. Somehow when you've grown up in the good old homogeneous Midwest, you do feel there's a lot more exotic world out there somewhere."

"Hey, let me tell you, there's a pretty exotic world in the halls of Chicago public schools!"

"I'm sure you've got some wild stories, too. Some of us got our fill of exotic during the war. The campaign in Italy did a lot to cure my romantic dreams about that part of the world. Ten months of slogging through Italian mud and dust will do that for you!"

"I imagine so. But the Army was mighty glad to have some of you Sons of Italy to help out during those war years. Speaking of the war, now that it's behind you a few years, do you feel as though you're settling back into normal life."

71

"Yeah, I finally feel like I am. Marrying Lucy helped a lot. And landing my job at Boston University."

"Are you enjoying your work there?"

"Yeah, they gave me a half-time assignment this semester so I could finish up my dissertation. That's one reason I could take a few days out here with my mom. I'm doing some work over at the University and Art Institute libraries. Hey, I forgot to ask Judith. Is she in the Ph.D. program at the University?"

"No. You know by the time she finished her Master's there, she was really fed up with academic politics."

"I remember that. She had a real feud going with old Villeneuve. I think he was ready to throw her to the wolves. LaChasse saved her thesis, I know."

"Whatever got her in so bad with Villeneuve?"

"There were a couple of things, but it started one day in a Modern French Lit. class. I remember it so clearly. Villeneuve was carrying on about the roots of some modern poetry and claimed that the whole 'carpe diem' theme related to Villon. Well, Judith knew it wasn't Villon, it was Ronsard and some of the classics before him, so she corrected Villeneuve in front of the class. Instead of just admitting he'd made a mistake, he tried to bluff it out and you know how stubborn Judith can be, knowing she was right, she wouldn't back down. Villeneuve never forgave her for making him lose face and then it turned out he was on her Thesis Committee. Big trouble."

"I can only imagine. Well, I know it left her with a bad taste in her mouth. She felt a lot of people she'd trusted had betrayed her in order to cozy up to Villeneuve. I guess she was lucky to get out with her M.A., and she won't consider going back there. You know how it is around here, if you're not going to go to the university, where are you going to go?"

"Hey, Chicago has lots of good places. She could go to Northwestern, couldn't she?"

"Yeah, I think she has considered that. But between her fulltime teaching and Pat's health and then worries over her mom and aunt, I think she's finding it hard to get back into the academic life. Oh, yes, and besides that, now she and Pat are talking about moving out west."

"WHAT?"

"Yeah. Remember Trudy Swenson?"

"Sure. That tall blond gal in the WAC who was teaching pilots geography or something during the war?"

"Yeah. Well, she and her folks moved out to Washington a couple of years ago, soon after Trudy got out of the Women's Army Corps. Judith and Pat took a trip out there to visit them last August. They visited the mountains and the beach and now they're just crazy about the Northwest. Pat carries on and on about the trees. I say to him, 'Hey, Pat, we've got trees. I mean what are all these elms?' But no, no; it's the *fir* trees Pat loves. He says elms spend seven months of the year looking like skeletons, while fir trees are always green, even in the depths of winter. Therefore, Washington's and Oregon's fir trees are more *hopeful* than Chicago's elms. 'Didja ever hear the like?' As me auld mither would say."

"Gosh, I can't imagine Judith leaving Chicago. Surely, they're not seriously thinking of moving. They just bought a house."

"Yeah, well, they'd started that deal before they visited out west. Judith had a little money from her dad's life insurance and they have agreed they won't rush into a move west. Judith had just accepted this Loyola College job, too. She thought she should honor that contract for at least a year or two. Her Mom hates the idea of their moving 1500 miles away, so Judith's kind of torn. Actually, I suspect Pat likes the idea of putting some miles between them and the family. He's probably thinking of poor old Henry. Anyway, in these times, you can't go wrong buying a house, even if you sell it a year later."

"Well, that's sure true. Prices are going up so fast you can practically hear them, like corn growing on a summer night."

"Ah, Tony, I'm happy to see Boston hasn't taken all the Midwestern similes out of you!"

"No, no. You can take the boy out of Chicago. . . What about you, Mary? Do you ever think of trying out some new places? Several of my army buddies have moved out to California and they're crazy about it."

"I know. My brother Damian moved out to San Jose after he left the Air Force. And Eileen's husband is badgering her to move to Los Angeles. But for me, I don't know. Chicago just seems like home. Besides, what would I do without the entertainment of Chicago politics?"

"Oh sure. Are you still one of the stalwarts of the North Chicago Democratic Women? I can still remember how revved up you and Judith and Elizabeth could get over the cause of a good Democrat."

"Well, Judith doesn't make it to as many meetings as she used to, but she's as faithful a Democrat as ever. At the New Year's Eve party, someone had let a Republican or two in and one of them, not knowing Judith, had dared to ask somewhat disdainfully, if she was a Democrat. Something along the lines of, 'You're not a Democrat, are you?' That guy sure didn't know the crowd! Anyway, Judith drew herself up to her full five feet two inches, looked down that up-turned nose and said coldly as only she can, 'Of course I'm a Democrat. I'm a working woman,' and she proceeded to provide him with examples of what Republicans had NOT done for workers or women. That guy retired into his bottle of beer in a hurry!"

"Well, listen, Mary, it's been just great talking to you, but I'd better let you go. My mom's phone bill will be awful and I'll have to take out a loan to pay it."

"Oh, no, luckily North Chicago still has the local call system. If they go to charging by message units, it will sure cramp the style of a lot of talkative Maloneys. But, yikes, I hadn't looked at the clock. I've gotta run, too. It's been great talking to you, Tony. Give my best to your mom."

"I will. And say hi to your family for me. Next time I'm in town maybe we can get together."

"We'll plan on it. Bring Lucy next time. Thanks for calling, Tony."

"Great talking to you. Bye, Mary."

7

LOVE LETTERS
Spring and summer 1943

Sherman, Illinois
Tuesday, April 20, 1943
Dear Trudy,

We'll have to do <u>something</u> about writing. It seems so terribly long since I saw you. I don't know where to begin.

Much has happened since I wrote last. Last week my landlady Vera Barker's brother came home on furlough. She had talked about him quite a bit, but I wasn't at all interested since I had just about decided to marry Joe. I saw the brother for about three minutes one evening when he came over (his parents' home is in St. Charles) just long enough to be introduced. Three nights later he called to ask for a date. I accepted without TOO much pleasure; so, Friday night he called to take me to dinner in Aurora.

Well, we started to eat about six o'clock. By eleven we were engaged.

Saturday evening, we went out again and Sunday morning I took him to the train and he left for his camp in Denver. Do you remember last winter when you said you thought that love was something like a tidal wave? I don't think you used those words, but I think that was your idea, n'est-ce pas? Anyway, that is what happened to us. After only a few days we felt sure we were meant to be together.

The thing that first attracted me was his sense of humor. (Mary Maloney would approve!) He exaggerates more than I do!

Further details: Pat is six feet four, weighs 200 pounds, is dark, was once voted the outstanding young man of St. Charles (we keep that quiet,) is a very good artist and is much interested in music, an ex-tennis champion, a good skier, and has an Irish father and a Swedish mother. Age: 30. Profession, currently, First Sergeant in the Army, Camp George West, Golden, Colorado.

I shall write soon and further if you will write me just a little note telling me about yourself. Please, Trudy.

Love,
Judith Jensen

Golden, Colorado
April 21, 1943
Wednesday Evening

Carol, Darling . . . . . .

If ever I've missed anyone in my life it is now and it
is you. After the few wonderful hours that I spent
with you, coming back to something like this is not easy.
The whole company was in an uproar when I arrived (not
because I arrived.) Remember my telling you of our
Company Commander whom we all thought so much of?
He, unfortunately, has left us and his place has been
taken by a Lieutenant whom everyone dislikes with
enthusiasm. Everything is upset and the chap I left in
my place didn't do a very good job, so I've had a lot to
do since Monday. This is the first chance I've had to
write to you, dear, and this only because the rest of
the company is at a camp show tonite.

Enough of this—I can't tell you how anxious I am to
get the first letter from my darling. It's going to be
grand getting letters from you. This in spite of the
realization that every word from you will make me
soooo anxious to be near you.

You know, sweet, I've never wondered for a moment
whether the whole thing was real or not. I had assumed
that after getting back here and being able to think
about it all that, perhaps, I would ponder upon whether
or not we moved too quickly. In spite of really trying to
reason things out there's something so fine, so
wonderful, so natural about our affair that there's no
doubt about anything. This is it. I know it. My heart

and my mind both agree. And it all makes me happier than I had imagined I could be.

Trying to pretend, darling, that from now until after school is out isn't such a long time to wait for you but I know that it is—no use pretending. It's going to be almost unbearably long. After years of waiting for you the few months left will seem longer than all those years.

Just as soon as I find time to get downtown, I'll see about a ring, sweet. Then immediately after payday I'll have something besides letters to send you. Furloughs are quite the thing. I should have tried them before. Now I want another so I can get engaged to you again. I wonder how long I would have gone on living and thinking I was happy if I hadn't met you, dear. A contented sort of happiness is one thing and ecstasy is really something else. I'll take ecstasy.

From now on everything I do will be for you, darling. And because of you.

How are you getting along since Sunday, dear? I guess I rather forgot something—dropping by for you without thinking of how you were to eat that day. I'm so sorry—thoughtless of me, wasn't it? I can't be thoughtless and careless from now on and that's about the only thing I'll miss about bachelor life.

I sat up all night on the top of my Lincoln-Zephyr, watching the moon travel westward and thinking of many things. Most of those things were connected with you.

How about your own reactions, dear? Are you still as happy as you seemed when you were in my arms?

Does it seem like a long, long time until school is out for you, too? Are you still undecided about this summer? Do you think you could put up with me for the rest of our lives?

So far, we have heard nothing authentic about the immediate future of our Company. I'm still trying to discover what they'll be doing with us and I'll let you know as soon as I do.

The gang is coming back from the show and will be crowding the Orderly Room to get passes, so I'll let you go now, sweet. If possible, I'll write again tomorrow and between writing to you and receiving letters from you, I think I'll be able to get along somehow.

Take care of yourself for me, darling. I love you so much and want you exactly as you are (unless you insist upon getting your hair cut.) Be good to your Spanish students and let me know what your friends think of your change of status. Maybe you won't tell them until the ring comes?

And write soon, darling.

All my love. . .

. . . Pat

Golden, Colorado
April 25, 1943
Sunday evening

Gorgeous. . .

Poddon the pencil and poddon the paper. Reason: came over here to Jennie's for a beer and a peanut butter sandwich on toast and to write to you but I just discovered I left my pen on my desk back at camp.

How are you, darling? As lovely as when I left you? You didn't cry before I left (and I'm glad) but did you after I was on the train and the train pulled away?

How soon are you going to send me a picture, darling? So that I can make the boys see how it was possible for their old Sarge to fall so hard and so fast. Besides, I really need a picture—not having you near.

I severed connections with several feminine friends the last couple of days, sweet. Terribly honest I was about it, too, and they liked me for it. I'm living for you alone now, dear. The guys have noticed it also. Not that I'm making such a radical change as to appear ridiculous—too old and established for that.

I talked to the folks on the phone. Gert, my mother, seemed almost convinced by the time I left and, by now, is, I hope, thoroughly convinced. She's so used to my being single and occasionally interested in some girl that she hardly thought I could be serious about a new girl in so short a time. Well, hell (poddon-that happens to be one of my favorite expressions—probably because it rhymes)—it's hard to believe it myself, precious. But believe it I do. It's just as natural as breathing.

Here in camp we prepared all last week for a "problem" on Saturday. There were many rumors concerning it. One of them turned out to be correct: our battalion was picked by 7th Service Command Hq at Omaha to be the Military Guard for our Commander-in Chief—FDR in his inspection of Fitzsimons Hospital and Remington Arms Plant in this area. It was considered an honor in view of the fact that there are so many thousand troops around Denver. We did a good job, too, Sweet. An Intelligence man, with the Pres., told "Big Red", our Battalion Commander (Bn Comdr) that our job of guarding was as good as he had seen in his travels with FDR.

Finally got the MR, DSK BK, and DRtr (Morning Report, Sick Book, and Duty Roster) (WDAGO Forms # 1, 5, and 6, respectively) (I'll drive you mad with GI language, my love) in shape again. They were rather badly messed up during my leave.

If some pix can't be sent by you to me soon, sweet, how about a snapshot to hold me until you can send one? I gotta have something besides the most wonderful memories of something so sweet that poor Murray can't adequately describe the resulting reactions.

All I know, lil heart-throb, is that a tidal wave engulfed me (No-I did not read that in a book!) And the grandest thing about it all is that I know it's not youthful "infatuation" that might have happened several years ago.

10 min later

Back in the orderly room.

To know that this, what I had told myself over and over again would never happen to Murray, has happened. I'm not childishly overcome by it all—neither am I the least bit casual about it all. I'm just immensely delighted to know that this is love. I love you terribly, darling.

Naturally, sweet, I can think more calmly about this thing when I'm away from you than when I'm near you and yet, strangely enough, I continue to arrive at the same conclusion: that Carol and Pat should be married as soon as school is out this spring. If you now have different ideas let me know. I know so little of your situation, darling. Your home ties and so forth. I am absolutely certain that we can iron out any difficulties that arise. Don't you agree? I love you so much that nothing else seems to matter.

Take back that statement, partially. Because of you, sweet, everything else seems worthy of more effort. This job of mine f'r instance. Because of what you mean to me, I'm working harder than ever at it. Other things, too.

Had my "last fling" last nite, dear. You won't mind, I know. From now on you'll become part of everything I do. S'matter fact, darling, you have been ever since I met you. Can't help it. Don't wanna help it.

Should write to my sister so you won't mind too much if I leave you now?

Perhaps the next letter will be more informative and will have less of this outpouring of sentiment, but this, and you, are so new to me I'm still a bit delirious. You don't object?

Take care of yourself for

Pat

Sherman, Illinois
April 26, 1943, Monday evening

> *So far, I have read*
> *Your lovely letter*
> *Over some fourteen Times*

> *One hour after having read*
> *your letter which arrived last week*
> *when I was in Chicago for Easter.*

Dearest,

When your train left, I felt as if I were completely alone on the face of the earth, but soon after I began to feel as I do now, that every moment I am becoming more and more a part of you, not by any physical act of union, but by my intense love for you that continues on, strangely enough (or maybe, naturally enough) as if we were together every instant. I'm trying to express a feeling that I've never had before: that I feel so very close to you, even though I miss you achingly. Sometimes you seem so close I can almost feel you. Sometimes I can see you looking at me the way you did when we were together, the look that moved me so much. Sometimes I can hear you and enjoy that rising inflection you give to the end of your sentences. I've never felt this way about anyone before and never dreamed I could. I know now I'm completely yours.

I suspect that Vera feels that this is largely physical. She hasn't said so, of course, but I do have a good <u>intuition</u> (that's how I got through eighth grade arithmetic). It certainly isn't with me and my same intuition tells me it isn't just that with you. The way I feel about you is something that isn't merely one thing or a group of factors that can be broken down for analysis, except that it includes emotional and spiritual as well as physical aspects.

I'm so sorry to hear about Captain Baker's (wasn't that his name?) transfer; I know how you admired him, so you may be assured of my active dislike for the unsavory lieutenant. That does change things a little for you, doesn't it? It would be wonderful if you knew about future moves of your company; we could make more definite plans then.

You should be happy to know that my mother is busy getting me a lovely pale blue satin housecoat with lavender flowers on it - it's all for you, really - <u>your</u> new housecoat!

"Mein Kampf aus Sherman" (not the book, the Real Thing, my fight I told you about) is progressing merrily; there's going to be some special teachers' meeting mainly on account of me. Last Wednesday my homeroom (which consists of thirty grubby little freshmen who meet once a week for a half-hour to discuss "common problems") was playing "What's My Name?" under my supervision when Primsky walked in and sniffed around. At that precise moment, we were doing Gypsy Rose Lee (I believe in teaching the intellectual approach to burlesque). He walked out frowning horribly. The bell rang ten minutes earlier than usual. There was a sign on our bulletin board "No more homerooms until special meeting has been held on subject" and Prim has since divulged to various people that Miss Jensen does not understand the true purpose behind homerooms, which is "to orientate the children in school."

I'm sorry I didn't answer you sooner, but I left here Thursday morning (Easter vacation you know) and evidently your letter arrived during that day or Friday, so I didn't get it until tonight. My Easter vacation was not a success physically; I spent it in bed with a strep throat, but mentally it was wonderful; I had nothing to do but think about you. I still have the infection (the strep, but also you) the first I've ever had, but I'm sure it will clear up soon. Vera and Quentin are taking good care of me. I have much medicine, and I'm not going to talk in class this week, just write directions on the board. It should be fun.

I've told Nan, my roommate, about us. At first, she wouldn't believe me for several reasons, but Vera finally convinced her. Darling, you will find enclosed a very awful picture of a sedate looking person; it is I. Just remember I don't always look that buttoned-up. Please write as often as you can and I shall write every day until you beg me to stop.

All the love that is or ever was,

Carol

P.S. Please forgive my horrible handwriting which is Fault no. 1: handwriting.

P.P.S. In each letter, I shall close with one of my faults.

P.P.P.S. I still love you as much as when I began this letter.

P.P.P.P. S. Dearest, if I sound egotistic and talk mainly about myself, it's because I'm trying to give you some idea of what I'm like. And some _warning_, also.

Sherman, Illinois
April 27, 1943

Pat darling,

I still love you as much as I did last night when I
wrote you. At this precise moment, my twenty-four little
freshmen boys (in English) are reading "How Santa Claus
Came to Simpson's Bar," so that I can tell you how much I
care. (The boy in the first seat in front of me evidently
suspects everything is not as it should be and is practically
cross-eyed from trying to keep one eye on his book and the
other one on this sheet of paper. Don't worry; he's an
illiterate, anyway.)

I have had a brilliant idea that will facilitate our
knowing each other's likes and dislikes; any day now you
may expect a twenty-page questionnaire something like
this: "Directions: check item 'T' if true, 'F' if false:

    1. ( ) I like pancakes.
       ( ) I do not like pancakes.
       ( ) I loathe pancakes.
    2. ( ) I liked "The Nutmeg Tree".
       ( ) Carol has rotten literary tastes. The book is
too corny for words.
    3. ( ) My favorite color is red.
       ( ) "   "   " blue.
       ( ) "   "   " pink.
       ( ) "   "   " yellow.
       ( ) "   "   " green.
    4. ( ) Carol talks too much.
       ( ) Carol doesn't talk enough.
       ( ) I guess she's o.k.

and so on.   I hope you will answer the questionnaire faithfully and honestly.

Darling, I have been thinking about us. After we get married, let's have fun, shall we, and not get stuffy like most married people? Let's take a year off sometime and travel, roughing it, on fifty cents a day! Wouldn't it be wonderful to hike through southern Spain and France and stay in little inns (or under haystacks), ride donkey carts in Sicily, and spend some time in Greece (I have lots of friends in Greece.) Of course, it would have to be after the war. The thing is I don't want to be 'soggy' the way most people are when they're married. That's why I want you; because I know you're not that sort of person. You are perfect.

Exclusively and passionately yours,

Carol

P.S. Don't work too hard—please.

P.P.S. Fault no. 2: I'm careless; I burnt up the electric stove that belonged to the woman I lived with last year. (I never have told Vera this.)

Sherman, Illinois
April 27, 1943
Tuesday evening

Darling,

I can see you wearily opening another of my letters and wondering whether you had better marry me after all to stop the deluge! (It *is* an idea.)

I forgot to tell you in the last letter that I like the way you walk (sorry I can't say anything about your legs), and the non-committal look you wear so often fascinates me. Maybe I don't like you after all, but am only curious to know what's behind it. Well, no, after thinking it over I believe I do like you, in fact, I love you intensely.

My day was wonderful today; I just sat without talking all day, since I can't talk very well because of the "strep," while my kiddies wrote and sweated. I believe I shall keep my throat condition until June so I won't have to work much. This evening Mildred (one of the very lovely-looking girls I work with) came over to hold my hand while I lay in bed. Suddenly she noticed your picture and became wildly enthusiastic about you, so enthusiastic that when she said archly, "You must like him very much," I replied *very* crossly, ": Of course, I do; I'm engaged to him," and then threw her out, for I noticed a predatory gleam in her eye.

Dear, I'm so lonesome for you tonight as I lie here writing, someone said today at lunch that she believed the war would last ten years at least. Really, I practically assaulted her; I don't believe I minded international conditions half as much as I did starting about a week ago.

Pat, it will be two weeks this Friday that we met; it doesn't seem that long, does it? It meant so much to me when you said that all our past is past and our future is together. That's how I feel, too. Any mistakes of our former lives have just been obliterated by the love we share.

By the way I have the little red bow in a glass case on my dresser next to your picture (which I look at the first thing on going to bed and on getting up mornings.)

Goodnight, darling

P.S. Fault no. 3: I exaggerate; I really didn't throw Mildred out.

Sherman, Illinois
April 28, 1943
Wed. evening

My home address in Chicago: 2730 N. Crawford Ave
In case you come home unexpectedly or the Barkers are swept away (like you) by a tidal wave.

Mon amour,

You have no idea how wonderful it is to come home after work and find a letter waiting on the dresser. I had a feeling that there would be one (a letter, not a dresser) but I was so afraid I'd be disappointed I refused to give in to the feeling. When we came upstairs, I let Nan go in first. I was afraid to look. (Darling in two weeks my whole happiness has come to revolve around you!) As soon as I saw the letter it took all my self-control not to push Nan away and to snatch up The Letter! I did read it before I even took off my coat or gloves or fascinator. Tomorrow I shall beam brightly at everyone.

Like you, I'm still delirious about it all, only this is a permanent kind of delirium. Certain of my friends should be very happy. For many years now, they have been unhappy over the fact that I have treated men cynically; I felt that I could never get emotionally tied up with anyone; physically, maybe, but never emotionally. I was going to marry money, and so on, and so on. Then my little friends would say, "Just wait, Jensen, when you fall, you're going to fall hard!" They were so right. I can see them gloating, but I don't mind.

Dearest, you keep getting in my way all the time; when I try to teach, there you are in front of me and the class; when I try to read, you are between me and the author, so I usually end up by putting the book down and talking to you. Every day at noon I think exclusively of you: the other teachers usually talk shop, so now instead of becoming nauseated, I appear to concentrate fiercely on the chow (for their benefit) while, thus protected, I contemplate you. I mean this darling; I'm not kidding.

Of course, I do kid a lot, but not where you're concerned. I hope you won't object to my tendency to take things lightly. I've learned to in the course of almost twenty-five years that would have been pretty grim without a sense of humor that, I admit, may have become exaggerated. Things started going awry when I was eight years old, when my father lost all his property and I used to pray that he wouldn't commit suicide because he had lost everything, and so on and so on. That was just the beginning of a string of things, a few of which I shared with you. But it is true about me: I haven't had too happy a life up to the last two years. I'm not complaining, but I do want to be careful about letting us into anything.

Darling, I want your happiness above everything; are you <u>sure</u> you're perfectly sure about marriage? Do you think that you wouldn't feel trapped when it goes on year in and year out? I realize perfectly that men give up more than women do when they marry, and you have been around. Do you think that it might be better to wait until another furlough so that you can look at me in another light, see me in different clothes, talk to me, <u>may be</u> kiss me chastely once or twice before taking the final step? You know: 1. I can't do arithmetic, 2. I exaggerate, 3. I am careless, 4. My omelets fall, 5. I am not very tall (although I am taking stretching exercises and practicing faithfully) 6. My fascinators are too outrageous, poised on my head like a bird's nest.

In answer to your question: I haven't seen your family since gloomy Sunday. No, I didn't cry until we got home. Your mother seems non-committal. I feel she's pursuing a policy of watchful waiting.

What did you mean by the statement that the men in your company have noticed a change in you? What do you do now: kiss them on both cheeks when they do something well, swear less, bathe more often, or read poetry? I am intrigued. I am also worried that you are working too hard; don't! Please take care of yourself, dear. I was really thrilled by your account of the good work your battalion did during F.D.R.'s visit. You know, I'd love to see you in camp ordering people around, but even more than that I'd love to be with you and be ordered around. I can't think of anything I shall ever want more than to be your subordinate, darling.

Please write me as soon as you can so that I can have the thrill of seeing a long white envelope on my dresser when I come home, weary, cross, and "homesick" for you.

Exclusively and passionately yours,
Carol
P.S. Fault no. 4: I don't keep up with current events.

Sherman, Illinois
April 29, 1943
Thursday evening

My darling,

Ninety-nine and nine-tenths of my time is still given over to thinking about you, and as a result, my disposition is becoming positively angelic; for example, I haven't kicked one dog or old lady this whole week. You're even influencing me in my literary tastes. I tried to read a mystery story this week and found I just couldn't get interested; I attribute this to my subconscious mind which approves of Sergeant Murray wholeheartedly and remembers that he said that he didn't like mystery stories. I can just see myself in two years, <u>completely</u> under your thumb, but loving it.

If you don't get any more letters from me, it won't be my fault; it may be that I shall be lying in some hospital. Why? Report cards came out today and a large percentage of the track team found itself disqualified because of "F"'s in Spanish. So tonight, after school I was practically mobbed by some of these people whom, however, I dealt with efficiently by handing out my usual line: that I had absolutely no interest in their progress, it's a business proposition with me purely, no work from them, no credit for them. Period! I acted very detached, very cold, and grimly impersonal, as they all flopped out dejectedly.

I am now sleeping with Mr. Barker's Japanese knife at my side, however. You see, my technique (as one sergeant to another) is not being tough or employing a rich vocabulary.

I just act terribly cold and impersonal and thus conserve my mental health.

I've been getting a lot of leads for jobs lately, one yesterday in Alton, Ill., near St. Louis, another today at DeKalb Township High School. But I don't know what to do until I know what your plans will be. If we were married when school is out, how will we work things? I know I had mentioned going to Mexico, but that was really pre-Jack thinking. I can't imagine going away so soon when I could be with you instead. Do I have to go? Could you live out of barracks and if you can't, what would we do? When we marry, I want to be near you so that I can see you often. Will that be possible? Then, a more delicate question, are you getting enough money to support me? And, in connection with finances, could I stay in Chicago until July and teach the first session of summer school? I would make enough extra money to be able to get a proper trousseau, which any proper French bride, or, better yet, improper, should have. I would be able to come out to Colorado toward the end of July. What do you think?

I shall now go to sleep and dream that I am in your arms, dear. (I hope I get a letter tomorrow.)

I love you
Fault no. 6: I like to eat...
In bed, and as a result...
Your secret pal in Sherman...
The sheets get covered with crumbs.

Golden, Colorado
May 17, 1943

Monday Darling

Evening, Carol. . .

(pardon. . . I'll start over)

Monday, Carol

Darling Evening. . . .

(just a bit nervous—I'll get over it)

Carol, Darling. . . .

(Ahh—here we go)

No! Yes! Yes! I agree completely and enthusiastically! Breaking down the agreement into its component parts we have the following:

No, precious, you do not have to go to Mehico this summer. What a stupid fool I have been!

How blind and unseeing (either is bad) you must think me! How woefully ignorant of me! Darling, the only reason I encouraged your trip across the border was because I thought you really wanted to go and I love you too much to stand in your way. I had imagined that you were looking forward to it and I shouldn't want to deprive you of any happiness whatsoever. Making you happy is going to be my most important mission in life.

So... if you really don't want to go, nothing could make me happier than to have you with me out here. I had thought it to be some sort of a splendid opportunity for you. But you're right, having you here for only a week or so and then having to part would be torture.

Yes—you can wait until July to come out here, dear. It will just be another month of slow death but if you can stand it I can. Seems so strange—my waiting so many years for you and now being so anxious because a few months must elapse before I have you in my arms. The practical reason, your teaching summer school for money for your wedding wardrobe, appeals to me. Up until I met you, I hadn't tried to save any money aside from bonds and insurance. The little discussion I had with the Jeweler wasn't on the house either. Speaking of the jeweler, I had another chat with the Railway Express Agent in Golden today and by now a package is on its way back east and should wind up in a day or two in Sherman.

I'm hoping you'll like it. I had the advice and assistance of a buddy, Sergeant Mike Sitters, who is one of our most experienced ladies' men. He assures me this ring, which was my favorite, is in impeccable taste. I wished I could be there to place the ring on the third finger of your left hand but I can't; so, you'll just have to understand that every bit of my love and every bit of me is with you at that moment. Make it a sacred moment, won't you, darling? I love you so much that I feel I'm actually with you at times and I want you to feel that especially when you open the package.

I have the wedding ring with me and it will stay here until you come west. It matches the one you're receiving, naturally, and I think it's quite something.

Yes—you can stay here until your school starts in September, sweet. Don't think I'm going to give you up until I absolutely have to. No, not me. What wonderful weeks those we'll spend together are going to be.

And so, it seems our plans are working out nicely. You're wonderful, dear. You really are. How can anyone be so willing to fit in with my plans? And I have a feeling that you and I will agree just as well in our whole scheme of living, dear. You're really wonderful, or did I say that?

Your boy is going, finally to Fitzsimons's Hospital tomorrow. Whether they'll force me to part with both tonsils, Leftie and Rightie, tomorrow or make me wait a day or three depends upon a preliminary examination. The arthritis and this miserable "spring" weather get along splendidly. This winter was truly wonderful but we are paying for it now for it has been dampish and coldish for over a week now. It has been snowing all day today, f'r instance. Which angers my arthritis and it, in turn, angers me. The pain is not acute, only maddening. If I could reach the lower regions of my throat, I would commit mayhem. But soon, I keep telling myself, my two tonsils and I shall part and I'll be a new man. Right now, I'm an old man.

Where would you work in June, darling? I know there are plenty of jobs open but I'm just curious. Curiosity is the nearest I'll ever come to jealousy, so make a note of that. I don't think I could be jealous. If it would please you, I could make a pretense of it but it wouldn't be authentic.

Saaay—the new position for next fall sounds wonderful. It really does. A very exclusive Private's Girls' School, she says. Perhaps it is different on the outside but here in the Army there is no such thing as an exclusive Private. And their girls are hardly exclusive, either. Or do I misunderstand youse? But, really, it does sound good. You'll be able to get home each nite, no? That will mean a lot, I know. The smaller classes and other advantages put Sherman High to shame, I think. Congratulations. Even the name of the School sounds wonderful. Names mean a lot to me, somehow.

Yes, I know exactly what you mean about married people getting stodgy, dear, and I agree entirely. Another thing that gets me down is this so-called "married talk" or that which young married people think it is their privilege to use before other young but unmarried people. More or less intimate things, often a bit off-color, sometimes really crude. It actually embarrasses me. I can't stand dirty stories in mixed company anyway and certainly can't approve of "married talk" if anyone I care anything about is present. So, let's not drift into that after we're married, shall we not? Good.

No, we'll not get stale and be staid conventional people. Not you and I, darling. We'll travel, we'll read, we'll play, we'll keep terribly alive. It'll be up to you to be the practical one in the family if we must have practicality at all. I'm sensible but not practical.

I think I must take a walk thru the snow to Jennie's, there to drink three glasses of beer and have a peanut butter sandwich on toast and come back to sleep and to dream of you. Won't you come along?

Yours. . . forever Pat

Sherman, Illinois
May 20, 1943
Thursday evening

Dearest,

It's the loveliest ring I have ever seen! It's absolutely exquisite! I was so thrilled when I opened the box that (please don't laugh) I began to tremble and I could hardly put on the ring. I had to use one hand to hold down the other while I showed it to Nan. Two hours later, writing at Nan's desk, I'm still completely shattered. I mean it. I am just overwhelmed. I don't know what to say except that I love you as I have never dreamed it was possible to care for anyone.

Of course, dear, I have felt that way since the evening I met you, but the ring, as you said, seems to make our marriage closer; I won't feel complete until then, dear, and I am utterly yours. That's why I'm so terribly happy about the ring. I feel as if I were closer, well, about in Omaha already, and then, the ring is so very beautiful. I love the three-stone arrangement and the square setting. Your taste is perfect, but then you are perfect. (Of course, I do send my thanks to Sgt. Sitters of the rich background of experience.)

I am anxious to meet your friends; they sound like fun. I can't wait until you meet my friends because some of them are great, Mary Patricia Maloney, for example, who is 5'9", quite burly, who mixes cakes efficiently, has millions of little relatives called Walshes whom she tells long stories about until you go mad, and has the most wonderful sense of humor. Maloney (you always call her by her last name) always worried so about me when I went with various men because she didn't think their sense of humor was sufficiently developed. She's dying to meet you and look you over. The Irish family name helps a lot!

I was glad to hear your reaction to my suggestion that I spend the summer near you. Really, I just don't see the point of being with you a week or two; I'd feel as if I had been divorced if I couldn't be near you as long as possible after our marriage, till school starts, at least.

You know, contrary to what most people might predict, I think our kind of marriage should be more successful than most. Most people, when they get married know each other so well that they take each other for granted; and familiarity has put a sort of glaze over their eyes so they can't really see each other the way they should. Darling, I shall never take you for granted. I can't wait to just look at you again. When you actually speak to me, I shall probably faint in sheer ecstasy.

I'm so worried because I haven't heard how the tonsillectomy turned out; I didn't even eat dinner tonight. And that should indicate how I feel; you know how much food means to me. But you do mean more. As soon as I get a letter from you that has good news I shall go out and throw my arms around the first stranger I meet and tell him or her, "Now I am happy again!" Really, I'm so worried that I don't see how I ever felt happy in my past life, B.P. Before Pat.

I hope you're well!

I am going to see a jeweler in Aurora tomorrow about having my ring sized. (I have very small fingers.) Vera has had some lovely work done there, so I can trust them.

Everyone thinks the ring a dream (they think it's just my type and laud you as a very discriminating person.) Of course, I don't think they fully realize the significance the ring has for me. It is like a magic circle that encloses only you and me in the most thrilling and wonderful of enchantments.

    Yours in the daylight and dark,
Carol

Fitzsimons, Colorado
May 26, 1943
Wednesday Noon

Carol, Darling—

This is my fifth attempt to write this morning. If I tear up this one, too, I'm going to give up the whole thing as a bum job. Can't seem to concentrate for some reason or other.

No letter yesterday, either. Sorry but I didn't get around to it. The doctor, Major May, an intern, and two nurses had quite a session persuading tonsils Leftie and Rightie to come out of their hiding place. Took more than an hour to do so. The chap before me was in there just nine minutes, so you can see what a stubborn sort of a husband you are going to have, dear. I'm the same way about money.

Today my throat is somewhat sore but not as bad as I thought it would be. The arthritis is no better but should be in a couple of days. So, I'm quite happy about the whole thing. Everyone should have a tonsillectomy just for a gag. I mean it really is a gag with eleven instruments, one of the nurse's hands and both of the doctor's in one's mouth at the same time. The doctor and the nurse were in love, I guess, for I'll swear they were holding hands for fifteen minutes at a time.

Then back to bed where one exists on milk, ice cream, cold soup for three or four days. On the third day, you go to the lab where an impression is taken of your throat so that artificial tonsils may be made for you.

Can't seem to concentrate today, dear. Perhaps I'll do better tomorrow. Can you love me as much without my tonsils as you have before? It doesn't seem to change my feelings. I am still quite insane about you.

All my love,

Pat

Chicago, Illinois
June 17, 1943
Thursday night

Dearest,

Right now, I want so terribly to be with you that I seem to have run out of words. You know, there are moments like that when some desire is so strong that it can't be translated into words; I feel that way now (Maybe if I begin to write, I shall become more articulate.) Only I think of you constantly, no matter what happens, I always wonder how you'd react and whatever I see, I want you to see too; I share everything with you, but I do wish it were with a more tangible you.

I'm so happy that you're going to finally leave your old alma mater, Fitzsimons Hospital! Let me know at once, won't you, when something definite is promised? The news of your chest x-ray was wonderful coming after yesterday when I reached an inexplicable low in discouragement and I was having visions of a hospital wedding with ward boys holding thermometers over our heads, nurses throwing cotton balls instead of rice.

Today I was substitute teaching at Burbank. I left everything in a state of chaos. First, I must tell you all about the Air Raid drill yesterday which I messed up (Necessary explanation: the children are supposed, when the bell rings, to go immediately to certain assigned places in the first-floor corridors and to stand in certain positions, normal positions, in complete silence until another bell rings.)

Yesterday when the first bell rang, I had to first scream at Salvatore Malano to stop throwing his paint water at Alessandro Farzullo and to threaten Joe Volarmo with suspension if he wouldn't come in from the window ledge, and to yank Vincenzo Vitelli out of the cabinet where he was stealing pencils. This took some time and finally I noticed the horrible silence in the halls, where people were standing at attention. In desperation, I told my kiddies to go to their places, so some went one way, and others in another direction, screaming. It was at this moment that the Supervisor of Air Raid Drills, Mrs. Ryan, came down to my end. I crept into the shadows, hunched my shoulders, and hoped she would think I was one of the 8A students. But she recognized me as Air Raid Drill Enemy No. 1.

Today I almost messed up the 8A graduation play because I couldn't decide who had paid to go and who hadn't. A slip of paper was handed to me with certain names checked; I couldn't tell whether the checks meant "paid" or "not paid" and the kiddies all insisted they had paid; bedlam ensued, with the checked and unchecked swearing at each other in Italian and insisting they had paid. Every two seconds I would bellow, "I want quiet in here! If I hear another sound no one is going to the play!" This statement would undoubtedly have been very effective if it could have been heard.

Then in the midst of this charming scene of happy, spontaneous youth, two angry teachers, Mrs. Hogan and Miss Quinn, strode in and bellowed to the poor, hunted creature that was I, "Miss Jensen, we have been waiting ten minutes for your class to come in to the play. We can't wait another minute to ring up the curtain!" I tried to explain that I didn't know who had paid and was eligible to go. Finally, between them, Hogan and Quinn discovered the truth, collected the money from everyone, and marched us, very meek, into the Assembly Hall where I sat down and tried to relax.

Meanwhile I noticed certain boys of my group being yanked out of the audience by Mrs. Kelly, but thought nothing of it. I discovered later that I had neglected to erase the names of those who had paid at the last minute (if they hadn't paid, they were supposed to remain with Mrs. Kelly). All these people had been rounded up in the office to receive their official suspension for having entered without paying. Of course, I explained. . ..

Then the milk money is in a terrible state; they get milk every morning and I'm supposed to collect the money and list the names. All week I collect the money, put it in my own purse, lose the names, and then when the milk arrives, everyone claims the milk and I pay out of my own money and then the boy who was to bring the money down to the office this week says he lost the money ... Oh, God!

Then the money for Defense Stamps which they bought today! Everyone dashed up, threw money at me, Ernesto Leoni dropped a bottle of red tempera on the floor, Amadeo Castellani, wanted "to go batroom", Nishian Doumenian wanted change for a quarter, someone came in from the office for the monthly attendance report, Giulia Troleta wanted to know if she could lead the "Pledge of Allegiance" next week instead of Esther Sciapetti who was a rat and was spreading the rumor that I was engaged to the boys' gym teacher, and John Cattalina was trying to rape Rose Larabedian (who seemed to be enjoying it.) All this while I was trying to put down what kinds of Defense stamps, how many, how much had been paid, etc. for the office. After I sent in the request for stamps, the office sent up word that I had sent down more money than was needed for the number of stamps I asked for.

This will go on tomorrow and next week. But it's buying, bit by bit, my trousseau, darling.

Darling, if you only were here; I don't think I can wait.

Exclusively and passionately yours,
Carol

Chicago, Illinois
June 29, 1943
Tuesday evening

Mi adorado,

Tonight, I went to the library to look up hypotrophic arthritis; all I could find was "hypotrophic: asymmetric growth of the radial organs." Holy Mother of God! Does that mean your arms and legs are growing in opposite directions? You're not growing into an octopus, are you? Darling, I love you and I love to be in your arms (2!)

Vera mentioned, in her letter, that the doctors said it was kidneys. Isn't that pretty serious? I worry more about that than about asymmetric growth of your radial organs. Really. I am worried. If I knew you would take care of yourself, I wouldn't worry so much. Tell me, do I have to worry? (All right; I'll change the subject.)

Darling, I was just wondering. When you mentioned spending part of your pass from the hospital at the City Park. Do you, too, often get awfully tired of people? Every so often I do like to be alone. Up to now I have always liked to walk alone at night (a habit which makes my family nervous.) May I walk at night after this with you?

Your fishing camp experience. I've had similar experiences: odors usually call up in my mind former experiences very vividly.

Have you ever read Marcel Proust's <u>In Search of Lost Time</u>? It deals with that kind of phenomenon better than anything else. Proust has a theory that the kind of recalled experience you had is more real, more vivid, more alive, than the original experience itself.

110

Today I was teaching at the Burbank. I was supposed to be teaching art and music! I went to the principal with tears in my eyes and said I would have to leave: I couldn't keep on stalling with the music much longer. He informed me that he simply wanted someone to be there to stand over the classes and what I taught was immaterial to him. He said in desperation, "What did you teach in Sherman?" "Spanish," I said apologetically. "All right, then, teach Spanish!"

So, I'm teaching Spanish now to my Italian kiddies and getting along all right. Since I speak Italian, they feel that I am kosher. By the way my predecessor is quite ill with inflammation of the nerve ends caused, I am told, by my boisterous Italians. By the way, I get along beautifully with Italians. I like them and they usually approve of me. When we are married, I hope our twins, Alice and Rex (Please, Sgt. Murray, I had planned on calling them Maltose and Dextrose, with Italian pronunciation: Mal-to-say and Dex-tro-say.) will be Italian because I do like Italian children. The names of my kiddies are wonderful, especially "Rizzi Rizzo."

You asked about my aunt. Aunt Minnie, my mother's older sister, is a very important person in our family; we live with her. She believes food is the most important thing in the world, and no matter what my trouble is, she runs out and buys me a box of Fanny May chocolates.

Darling, you said in your phone call that the words of the "Song of Songs" and parts of the Rubaiyat were ours. I agree completely; I read both tonight since I always keep them around, but tonight they took on a new and wonderful meaning. Reread them, won't you, again, and

111

feel that they say what I should like to. And the next time you hear, "You'll Never Know" on the radio, imagine that I am singing it to you. If I could sing.

Completely and unreservedly yours,
Carol

Chicago, Illinois
July 6, 1943
Tuesday morning

Dearest,

I am so discouraged! Here I put airmail stamps on your letters and pludge (combination of plod and trudge) across bridges that open in the middle (they terrify me!) so that you will get my letter in two or three days! And do you get them? Apparently not. Early in life I lost most of my ideals, but I admit I did believe in the ideal of the U.S.A. Air Mail... I hope by this time the Air Mail people have given up the two letters I mailed last Saturday, July 3.

I rated two letters today: your 5 p.m. Sunday one and the Monday one. Imagine! The Monday letter arrived this morning.

By now I hope my letters have convinced you how I feel about a discharge: I hope like everything that you may be put into limited service, but if you're not, I know you well enough to believe that in the Army or out, you are serving. Of course, I realize, don't think I don't, that you liked your job and I realize that you liked the Army life, so that I hesitate to say any more... I know there are times when words can be annoying and futile... But I think you know my opinion: My whole criterion is usefulness; I don't think you have to be in the Army to be useful. If you should remain in the Army and develop more arthritis as a result, you would not be useful; that seems to me simply a subtle form of sabotage. I do think the Army should take your past record into consideration and find something for you. I do appreciate how rapidly you advanced, and so does my family, if that means anything to you.

I'm so glad your radial organs are not growing asymmetrically.

By the way, Re: Stanislaus our seventh son, may we call him by his Polish nickname, "Stash"? And may we call our eighth daughter Zosh? (Nan's sister's name is Zosh.)

All the love there is or ever was,

Carol

Chicago, Illinois
July 13, 1943
Tuesday evening

Darling,

At 2:31 p.m. today I was visited by a horrible thought: maybe Murray is going to go down in history as the "Forgotten Man of Fitzsimons!" Therefore, I was terribly relieved to get your wire at 3:34 p.m. I couldn't help thinking all this morning how hellish it must be for you to be in that place waiting. . . It won't be so bad now, will it, now that you know definitely? For the first time in a week, I dared to look at the calendar. We'll have August together, won't we? Now that I have definite information on when to come, I'll ride hell-for-leather downtown for train reservations! I won't mail this letter until I have them in my hand. The rest of the plans I leave up to you. Incidentally, do you want to get married the same day I arrive? It would seem perfectly possible, wouldn't it? There isn't any residence requirement, I believe you said.

Thank you for your promptness in returning the food preference chart. I admire your honesty if not your tastes. I'm still not won over to the idea of peanut butter on toast. And how is it that macaroni appeals to you and not spaghetti? (She asked, puzzled) Hmmm, Garlic. Did I ever tell you how I broke up a beautiful marriage which had just started? On the Garfield Park El I told Rosella how to fix lettuce salad as it should be fixed, in the French fashion: break up the lettuce, pour olive oil over it, then some vinegar and salt, and lastly grate several cloves of *garlic on it. . . Rosella's husband has never felt the same toward her, it seems. (But the salad is good that way.)*

To be continued after Train Reservations Are Obtained.

Whadda day! At 8:02 this morning I re-read your letter. 8:05 I laid it down, 8:05-8:07 I bathed, ate breakfast, brushed teeth, combed hair, dressed, 8:07-8:15 looked for money (that took some time.) 8:10-8:15 I went downtown to the Northwestern Station with Mother and stood in line with five thousand civilians and fifty thousand servicemen, all wanting reservations.

The next time I try to make reser. (When am I coming? Please don't interrupt) as I was saying, the next time I'm leaving Mother home. She kept jostling everyone and saying to me, "Go on, slip in there, she's going to leave soon-go on, get in there," digging her elbows in sundry ribs all the while. After an hour, there was a small group preparing to lynch both of us. Fortunately, the agent reached me in time. Mother kept making remarks about how slow he was: "Why don't you go to another window? You'll never get waited on here, etc. (So, he hated us, too!)

Maybe that was why he told me the first reservation I could get was August 4!!! Unless I took my chances on one of the unreserved trains and changed at some place called Shy-Ann. That made me nervous! I had visions of scrambling out of the train at 2 a.m. at Shy-Ann and being stampeded while the Denver train left with hordes of people hanging out of windows and lying on the roof, and my suitcase gone forever. I declined to try my luck with the masses (When am I coming? Wait!) and left the Northwestern Station.

116

After going through the same jostling procedure at the Union Station, I learned that the earliest reservation he could give me was August 9: since I was too weary to go back to Northwestern, I accepted it, so there it is: August 9!

Did I say August 9? I'm sorry, I must have made a mistake; the Burlington people gave me a reservation for July 27 on the Zephyr (I'm not kidding now.) I doubt whether the Rock Island could do any better, so I left it at that. That means I arrive on the twenty-eighth and I have decided that maybe I had better rest one night in a hotel before trying on the matching gold band.

Oh, the cabin. It sounds MAGNIFICENT!!! (My family wants to come, too.) Don't give it up even if you have to defend it at the point of a gun. It sounds just perfect.

I love you so madly that I don't see how I can wait. Oh, darling, if I could only talk to you instead of writing! Mother appreciated your letter very much. Her own marriage was really a marriage of convenience and there was never any real love there. I am all she has, so she is understandably concerned about my future. Happily, she approves of you "wholeheartedly" by instinct, I guess, so she was happy about the letter. She says admiringly, "It's a lovely letter!" and swears she's going to keep it always. She told me she has a feeling she's "going to be proud of the marriage." I'm so happy, darling.

All the love there is or ever was,
Carol

Denver, Colorado
July 22, 1943
Thursday afternoon

Carol, Darling—

The first day of life On the Outside passed rapidly enough but today is dragging by. Awoke this morning at what I thought was the crack of dawn. Perhaps it was only a passing truck backfiring. But then a moment later I heard a cock crow! From reading, at an early age, stories about life in the country, I immediately associated the crowing of the cock with the rising of the sun. Wrong again—it was 11:30 a.m. and the rooster (no he hadn't overslept) was merely crowing because of another conquest—one of the younger things in his harem, no doubt.

So now, wide awake, I ran to the window (already open) and threw out my chest. After dashing outside to retrieve it, I came back in, took a shower, and went out for breakfast. Afterwards, I explored further the mysteries of ration points and sales tax tokens. It's enough to make me wish for the pointless and token-free GI way of living.

This place is very nice indeed but it needs you, darling; so do I. Perhaps we can get along until you arrive but we're not looking forward to that.

Your airmail special and a letter from M.P. Maloney were handed to me just as I was leaving Fitzsimons yesterday. I read yours while riding downtown. It was, as are all your letters, wonderful. What can we do to make this week go by faster?

The letter from your friend, Mary Patricia Maloney, was charming and congratulated me on the opportunity to give her dear friend "Judith" a proper Irish surname which she reminded me is always welcome in Chicago circles of power.

Tomorrow, perhaps, I shall go into town or up into the mountains. If the latter, I shall hitch-hike and go wherever the driver who pix me up is going. We used to do this in Missouri (Ozark Mtns) and Minnesota (Iron Ranges) but I hadn't in Colorado because I've been too busy. But I shall have to do something to make time pass quickly for I'm terribly lonesome without you, my love, and only the anticipation of seeing you soon helps. That does help tremendously, you know.

In a moment, I'm going to ask someone with a watch (mine hasn't arrived from home yet) if it's time to be hungry. It seems to be. So—tune in tomorrow for another thrilling chapter of "Life on the Outside" or "Live Alone and Loathe It."

Until then, Darling, take care of yourself until next Wednesday, and then I'll take over.

I love you, sweet—

Pat

Chicago, Illinois
July 25, 1943
Sunday afternoon

Dearest,

I find it difficult to believe that this is the last letter I'm writing you before we really belong to each other. It looks as if I'm leaving *AT LAST*. The dining room table at present is piled with: (1) manicure set, (2) XXX, (3) two dresses, (4) soap (my own special flavor), (5) a nightgown (my mother disapproves of it horribly on the grounds that it's indecent; she wants me to return it) (6) umbrella (7) two cakes of Baker's Chocolate (8) three doilies with tatting hand made by my French grandmother. Don't you think that the aforesaid articles could be classified in two categories: under (1) sacred and (2) profane love? (a phrase that has always puzzled me.) The Baker's Chocolate is a preliminary wedding present to you from my Aunt Minnie (chocolate is very rare here; I hope it isn't in Denver.) The nightgown (sorry, not black lace, but very sweet, mind?) is Exhibit no. 4 in my Plan of Seduction and Intrigue. On second thought I decided against black lace. Maybe I'm still rather timid (it's easy to be the head of a Seduction Plan on paper) sooO, I thought I'd match my mood. Give me a month of evenings devoted to double-features starring Jane Wyman and Marlene Dietrich so I can study their technique and then I shall indubitably wear black lace with much swagger.

What I'm really thinking about is how completely happy I am and how proud I will be to be your wife. It's true, I haven't known you long, but I've picked up enough *by deducing things from your letters, from things that Vera and her husband have said, and from being with you some twenty hours (that's the way I figured it: Fri. 6 p.m. - 3 a.m.; Sat. 5 p.m. -5 a.m.; Sunday 5 p.m. - 6 a.m. = 19 hours) to realize that, viewed objectively, you're a really fine person. I admire you terrifically and I respect you, something that is necessary for me in marriage. I'm tremendously fortunate, I know, and I shall try very hard to make you feel the same way. Nothing else will ever approach you, in my life. You are my life, Patrick Murray. These words are not rhetoric; I mean them. I probably won't say them again, or very often, but after my death if my heart were to be opened, I'm sure they would be found 'engraven' there.*

Until Wednesday then, dearest,
All my love forever,
Carol

Tuesday Nite (late)

I wouldn't be able to sleep tonite, I'm sitting up eating blueberry pie (bakery special) and drinking milk. And, very incidentally, thinking of you and what I can do to make you happy.

I'm writing this letter in case I become too flustered to tell you this—or I'm so glad to see you that I just sit (or stand) and stare at you. This is, of course, the simplest form of adoration. And I do adore you, darling, in every sense of the word. It isn't only because of your letters, though no finer literature has ever been written, but you know I fell (more of a power-dive) madly in love with you that first night. I believed in something and you turned out (a short prayer of thanks for Sherman High School) to be that something! I love you and that love is deep and inspiring, as well as being joyous, exciting, and altogether delightful.

By the time, you read this, I shall have met you at the station and we'll be at the cabin. TOGETHER.

Our country being at war makes many things a bit more complicated, but we'll take that fact in stride...

If today and in the days to come, you find things aren't as perfect as we'd want, then it will not be because I haven't tried to make them that way.

This afternoon, if you want to, we'll go back to town and get The License. We'll make arrangements for the pictures. We'll make reservations for the wedding breakfast.

And that's all for now, dear—why don't you get back in the kitchen where you belong?

My love until tomorrow

And then

All my love forever,

Pat

Pat and Carol were married Friday, July 29, 1943 in Denver, Colorado, and remained together till Pat's death in January, 1981.

8

THE HOUSE IN THE WOODS
Summer 1961

Carol and Pat's letters to Mary Maloney, Chicago, Illinois

Dear Mary,

I know I promised in our Christmas letter a full account of our house building adventures, and August has rolled around already and you've heard nothing. Pat says he can't be sure I'll give the correct and accurate version, so he is going to add a post-script; he says prepare for a lengthy one; to make up for any deficiencies in my account. Summer school is finished, Rex is off at a neighbor child's birthday party, and finally I have time to sit down and write you the letter you deserve.

Well, as you know, the suburban house we had when you visited us two summers ago, never quite suited us. It was a nice little box but just that. Now that I've been with Meriwether University long enough to be tenured, we felt that we were financially stable enough to do something about a house that would really be ours. In the pre-Christmas rush, I said to Pat, who had such a bad winter and was in the VA hospital more than he was out, "What would you like? What would make you happy?" He said, "A house of our own. A house in the woods." I said, "Then I will build you a house in the woods." It might sound a little impractical, but in the Northwest, it's really not. We're lucky here on the south side of town, there are still some wooded lots and if you don't insist on a view of the river, they aren't terribly expensive. We found a lot with some lovely old fir trees and a lot of beautiful undergrowth, vine maples and such. It's like something out of a *Pacific Northwest Scenic Sights* calendar!

We spent January and February drawing and re-drawing plans, working around Pat's hospitalizations, three times in those two months. (There were times we had blueprints scattered all over the VA's bedcovers, to the consternation of the nurses!) We had a great young architect who was willing to work with us and is still young enough to have reasonable fees. With his and our ideas and his expert input on relative costs, we were able to come up with a plan for a charming little house, innovative enough to suit us and conventional enough to be feasible, economically.

Getting financed by the bank was the hardest part. They really want you to build something like everyone else is building. What? The roof on that side will slant all the way to the ground? That is not how houses are built, it could affect re-sale! But finally, after negotiations, compromise, and a good bit of Irish blarney on Pat's part and French stubbornness on mine, we got the house loan we needed.

In March, during spring break, we were able to have the foundation laid and the building began. Our architect knew a young contractor who's a PE teacher and builds houses as his moonlighting job. (Do any of your Chicago *public school teachers want to try that? I'm afraid those Midwest winters wouldn't make it very practical!) He's a very hardworking and well-organized young man and he would schedule his crews for the week and then come over to the property every day after school to see how the day's work had gone. It actually turned out to be a very efficient system.*

We have enjoyed the process of putting our own ideas into the house and Dale, the builder, has a wonderful way about him. I would say, "We'd like to put a bigger window in the bathroom." Dale would never say no. He'd say, "Oh. Yes. We could do that. Of course, if we put a bigger window in the bathroom, we'd have to move the studs and if we moved the studs, we'd have to move that door and if we moved that door you wouldn't be able to open the hall closet. But if you really want a bigger window. . ." By which time, of course, we had got the point and realized the bathroom window was fine as planned. But some of our suggestions, like our many, many built-in bookshelves, he was very willing to accept and have given us great satisfaction.

The entrance to the house is quite private even though it is not far off the road. There is plenty of natural greenery to screen us nicely. With its asymmetric look (that long shingled roof on the east side that the Bank didn't care for!) and cedar siding, it looks both modern and natural in its woodland setting.

Then as you come inside, the interior is paneled, not with that cheap paneling people are putting in their family rooms these days, but with birch boards that have a soft glow. You feel almost as though you're coming into a mountain cabin, but we have all of our bookshelves, so at least you know that it's a mountain cabin where thinking people live!

The kitchen is small and there's a pleasant little dining room beside it where we can seat 6 or 8 people quite easily. The dining room furniture we were able to buy at an estate sale. That might make you think it's old-fashioned, but actually it's Danish modern, very sleek and modern. Pat and I agree that we don't want to feel we're back in Aunt Minnie's front room!

The south end of the house is almost completely glass and we cleared away enough of the trees so that good sunlight can enter there. This is important for a woodland house, as they can be dark and damp in the winter. Of course, the sun can get pretty bright and hot and we were able to find at an auction some fantastic drapes; they're a kind of a Klee-inspired pattern and were woven to order for the old Queen Elizabeth vessel probably back in the thirties. Very Art Deco, my dear. They're huge and cover all the windows; that will be a help in the winter cold, too. I'm sure you can imagine how it pleases Pat's romantic soul to have draperies that once graced the dining rooms of a venerable ocean liner!

There are two bedrooms upstairs. The upstairs is really a little loft built above the dining room and kitchen, overlooking the living room which has an extra high ceiling. (They call them cathedral ceilings but the term is far too grandiose for our little abode.) Pat enjoys the spacious feeling the raised ceiling gives. The rest of the house is rather small scale, so it's nice for him to have an area where he can really stretch that big Irish frame of his!

We finished up most of the details of the building in late July and actually moved in just after Rex's tenth birthday. He was thrilled to have his birthday party in the New House. There are some nice children in the neighborhood, so we're hoping that Rex will enjoy growing up here. He's such a bright boy, but it's not easy for him when I have to work long hours, especially if Pat's having a bad spell. I sometimes worry that Rex is beginning to turn a bit inward. As a little boy, four or five years old, he was so joyous and spontaneous. That seems to be changing; but I guess children do have to grow up. Even if their parents would rather they stayed small and adorable!

One of the things I enjoy about our new House in the Woods is that there's practically no yardwork. No lawn to mow. In our stay in the suburbs I would worry and fuss every April and May when the grass would begin to grow maniacally, as it does in the spring here in the Northwest, and the lawn mower wouldn't start. So now the thought of no lawn to mow brings a smile to my face! Pat is determined, of course, being Pat, to do a little improving on nature on our lot. Of course, bamboo must be planted. If you hear of Giant Pandas invading the Portland area, you'll know he went too far!

Well, Mary, I must close this as it's time to go pick up Rex. When are you coming out for a visit? I suppose it's too late to plan for this summer. You'll be taking up your position again with Chicago Public Schools. Or do elementary school principals even get any time off in the summer? I suppose very little, and knowing you, you probably take even less vacation than you're entitled to!

But next summer. Next summer for sure, Maloney! We have a lot of catching up to do.

I'll leave some space for Pat to fill in any blanks I have left. With love to you and all the Maloney clan,
Carol (aka Judith!)

Hi, Mary,

I don't know that Carol's left many blanks in the Saga of the House of Murray. She has a way of covering topics pretty thoroughly as your longtime acquaintance with her will tell you!

We really are loving our new house. It feels very private after the years in Suburbia with the neighbors and their barbecues just across the hedge. And, nice as old Rick and Janice were, we enjoy the feeling of having our own small refuge from the world and all its cares.

I do think Carol may have minimized some of the challenges of building the place: I notice she didn't mention the time the cement contractor poured a four-inch slab for the carport instead of a six-inch slab. Or when the painters used the wrong kind of sealer on the deck and it left footprints every time you walked on it for about two weeks. Or the fact that the kitchen stove had to be moved 3 inches before we could open the refrigerator door. But we are really very pleased with the final results of our planning and work and we look forward to your coming out and sitting on that deck (now properly sealed) in the summer gloaming, sipping a little Jack Daniels and retelling the old Chicago stories.

By that time my small bamboo grove should be ready for a preliminary inspection. The only other real addition I'm making to the lot is to put in a row of lilacs. I don't think you ever saw our lilacs at the other house. They always bloom around the end of April and the first of May and they were a real show. I used to love to fill the house with them for Carol's birthday. She said she knew it would be a good year when she got lilacs for her birthday. We discovered that the masses of lilacs inside brought on asthma attacks for Rex, unfortunately; so, after that we had to enjoy them out in the yard.

Carol mentioned how Rex is growing up. I guess every mother hates to see her little one setting out on the path that will eventually lead him away from her arms, but he's really one great kid and we're very proud of him. I notice she was modest enough not to mention that he was in the top group in ALL skills in his 4th grade class—top reading, top math, top science. I know my illnesses are not easy on him—and certainly not on Carol for that matter. I'm happy to say that I've been doing well the last two months, though. I'm hoping the docs have finally come up with a good balance of the Multitude of Medicines they manage my condition with.

Well, Miss Maloney—Carol tells me it's now Dr. Maloney! Congratulations! I'll close by seconding Carol's invitation to come out and see us next summer. It would perk her up no end: you know how much your friendship has always meant to her.

Hope all's well back in the precincts and pathways of Chicago and that you're keeping those rowdy Maloneys under control.

Love from us all,

Pat

9

REX
Saturday, December 8, 1956

On a wintry and rainy evening, when Rex was a four-year old child, Carol gave her son his bath and dinner. In his pajamas already, Rex was now ready to go to bed.

"Mommy, please, read me a story."

"Shall I read you Puss-in-Boots in French with the cat and his master the *Marquis de Carabas*?"

"No, Mommy, I want to hear it in English. Mommy, I hear noises on the roof."

"It's only the rain pitter-pattering on the roof, or a squirrel, maybe some elves, even. Maybe it's Santa Claus's helpers. Christmas is near. They have to practice to get ready for the holidays just as we do."

"Oh! Goody, I want lots of presents from Santa. But there's the noise again, Mommy. Listen. I saw a squirrel in the woods behind Rick's house yesterday. He had a tail like a lion and big claws like a bear. And he was green and orange. I'm afraid. I want a light in my room."

"Well, of course, we will put a night light, here, just near your bed. But there's nothing to be afraid of. Your daddy is here to protect us."

"But, Mommy, what if Daddy's sick? How can he protect us?"

"Don't worry; Daddy can protect you very well, even from his bed. We have that big baseball bat by our bed. And I will protect you, too. You know I can run very fast when I want to. You must sleep now, sweetheart. We are near you. Don't worry."

"Mommy, I need to go to the bathroom."

"All right, dear, I'll take you. Here, we'll turn the bathroom light on. That's a big boy. Now, back to bed."

"Mommy, will you read me another story?

"No, Rex, it's too late. You must sleep now. Good night, darling. Sweet dreams. *Fais de beaux rêves!*"

1961, Friday November 3

REX, 10 years old, sits calmly at his school desk, concentrating on the letter he is writing his father. He puts the address 'Pat Murray at US Veterans' Hospital,' in perfect longhand strokes with his special pen, the ink being of his choosing, color purple. The teacher walks between the children's desks to check the assignment she has given her pupils: 'Write a letter to someone you love or to an imaginary friend.' She leans over Rex's desk to check his work after he has finished recopying his rough draft and begins on the envelope.

Dear Daddy,

In cub scouts, I have got my bear and my beaver bar awards at the last pack meeting. Since you were not there to take me Thursday after school I stayed with the Carsons and went to the meeting with them and stayed overnight.

On Halloween, I stayed with them too. For dinner, we had cow's tongue, macaroni and cooked spinach. I got a really scary mask downtown and I wore a black cape. First, we started trick or treating around Fir Grove road then we trick or treated on River road. It was kind of spooky walking past the dark woods places. Then we went home to count our loot.

I am going to play my recorder at the Christmas assembly. A couple of days ago, the handle on my briefcase came off.

I am looking forward to when you can come home. I love you very much.

Cordially

Rex P. Murray

Sunday, June 17, 1962

Rex, eleven years old, has typed a letter to his father on his parents' home typewriter.

HAPPY FATHER'S DAY
Dear best father in the whole world,
Instead of sending you a card this year I am writing a letter instead.
Here are five reasons why I think you are the best father in the world.
1. You are always kind.
2. You are fair and honest.
3. You spend a lot of you're (*sic*) time with me.
4. You always try to make things very pleasant for me.
5. You take me to Little League games, buy me hot dogs and loan me money whitch (*sic*) proves you are the best father in the whole world.

REX

Monday, August 5, 1963

Rex, age twelve, writes to his parents a sloppy letter in pencil from his B'nai n'Brith Summer Camp.

Dear Mom and Dad,
     I apologize (sic) for writing in pencil but the pen is missing. This is really a neat camp. The lake is not too cold once you are in it. I had a swimming test yesterday and qualified as an intermediate. Guess what they had for lunch yesterday…lunchmeat sandwiches with musterd (sic) even. The cabin is nice and has lights. It is surprisingly big, because it holds 15 beds. We have two councilers(sic)just for our cabin. I met a nice boy in the lake and now we are friends and do everything together.
     Your loving son,
     Rex. Murray (Rex P. Murray)

Tuesday, July 21, 1964

My journal at B'nai n' Brith Camp,

I hate this rotten camp. Last year I did not like to go away from home, but I got used to it after a while. The lake was fun and I had a friend, at least, and we went swimming, played in the woods and went everywhere together. And the food was good. Lots of spaghetti and meatballs, sandwiches and stuff like that.

This year I hate it! I feel like an idiot and now I have to write to my two fellow idiots in Fir Grove. I promised them I'd write every day. I have a little quiet time now. It's rest period, in the afternoon so I'll drop them a note. I hate feeling so far away, even if it's only a two-hour drive from home. I'd run away but then they'd know I'm not brave and they'd worry if I disappeared. And they are so proud of me.

They think I'm perfect. Mother keeps saying she remembers how mature I was last year when I came home from camp, and she is sure the same thing is going to happen this year. She said she showed my last letter to her friend, Sue, because she thought it "exceptionally well composed." Both she and Dad worked on the school newspaper in their college days, so I have to keep up the tradition of being a good writer and I have to try to be interesting and funny, too. I know they expect me to.

Mother signed her last letter "The Belle of Fir Grove," And she is, too. Ma belle! But it's hard to have to tell your parents that everything's fine at camp when you want to scream that you're miserable. Mother said she left my light tan shoes out in the living room to make her and Dad feel that I'm still around. It was nice to hear that, but just thinking about it now makes me want to cry. Mother is learning to drive, but Dad is not teaching her.

He can't get out very much.

She is taking lessons from AAA in a clunky Ford station wagon. It will be fun when she passes her test and can drive us everywhere. Dad's health is getting worse and there are a lot of times when he can't drive. But I'll be able to go downtown with Mother more often when she gets her license. Poor Dad, he probably will be in bed all the time soon. I help mother in the kitchen, sometimes, and I make sure the counters are clean. It helps her when I clean the kitchen. Dad can't do many things around the house any more, not much in the garden and not even that much in the kitchen.

Mother said she had to plant the begonias herself. She's never been a great gardener, that's for sure. She was probably complaining the whole time. Luckily Dad can still pay the bills and stuff. That helps Mother a lot.

There's a good song playing on the radio. The Beatles! They're so cool! I wonder if Mother and Dad would take me to the new Beatle movie. Maybe we could go as soon as I get back. It's my birthday in two days. Rex Patrick Murray, born July 23rd, 1951, Chicago, Illinois. Yippee! It's really no big deal, I know. Mother said she sent me a package special delivery. I wonder what it is. I hate being at this camp, so far from Mother and Dad on my special day.

The counselors will bring in a stupid banner and a white frosted cake at lunch. I wish it was chocolate. And the whole rotten camp will sing "Happy Birthday!" Like they care if I have a happy birthday! I hate that kind of pretending they like you when I know most of the kids don't give a hoot about me. They hardly even talk to me. We exchange maybe two words, and then only at ping-pong! Well, I'd better write my letter. I'll try to sound cheerful. I don't want my folks to worry. Maybe I can make my letter a little funny.

Letter from Rex to his parents, a few minutes later.

July 21, 1964
Dear Paul and Ringo,
The weather around here is absolute garbage. For two days in a row it has rained almost constantly. On the baseball field, there's a pond a foot deep. I might feel like going for a swim on the field instead of in the lake. I am almost the best ping-pong player in the Camp this year. Only about two people are better than me. Today I beat a kid in ping-pong and won a candy bar. We betted. From now on I am a GAMBLING MAN!

Last night, we had a little scare with the threat of tetanus and lockjaw in one of the little kids. He was going to the latrine to throw up as usual after supper, which tells you something about the food here, and his jaws became locked. It was pretty funny. The counselors had to use a crowbar to open his mouth. Later, we had a visit from the County Health Department, of course. There was some more excitement this morning when Richard H. wet his bed (no kidding) and then he acted up all day. It will be nice to have as much food as I want when I come home (wishful thinking.) I can hardly wait.

You tell me being away from so many adults is wonderful for me, Dad. So, I won't complain about the kids here. I was glad you fell for my joke with the book that I left under my pillow. Wasn't it a good idea to put that "Mad" cover that looked like it was "Sex and Love" over Advise & Consent? And you found it yourself. I'm glad you liked my joke.

I don't sleep too well at night because I MISS YOU BOTH SO MUCH. I love to get your letters. I will try to send a letter every day. I can hardly wait to get back. I am going to that incongruous Congregational Church tomorrow. The only reason is if you go to church you get to sleep later, 8 instead of 7 a.m., and it's a chance to get away from the camp for a while.

Mom, be sure that you practice driving just around the neighborhood, and, please, ask people to stay indoors until the Civil Defense Authorities give an "ALL CLEAR" signal.
Love and Junk and Stuff
Your son, (in case you forgot) Dynamic Rex, the Head Cool Guy

Thursday, February 6, 1969

Rex's Journal at Andrews Preparatory School, Massachusetts

I cannot stand this cold anymore. It might be great skiing with all this snow, but it's too cold for me to even want to put my nose outside. These preppies are such idiots, laughing and screaming at each snowstorm as if manna was falling from heaven. They all cheer, rush out, grabbing their skates or their skis. They're going skiing this Saturday—the school runs a bus. Where is the nice Northwest rain, that sweet climate? At least it didn't snow today, even though it's freezing.

The snowstorm in Upstate New York was horrendous and a town near Lake Ontario had thirty-foot snow drifts on the main street. It was even 10 degrees down in Florida. The only skiing I want to do is sitting in front of a screen at a ski movie tomorrow night. I guess I will have to stick my nose outside to go to the theater on the other side of the campus. Darn it.

But Mrs. Chandler has also invited some of us to come to her apartment this weekend to watch Batman on TV. I hear it's a terrific show and I can't wait to see it. I couldn't go last week because of my cold, but I guess there were twenty seniors squeezed everywhere in her place, spread out on the floor around her TV. I won't miss it this time and I have to say old Chandler is a pretty nice lady to have us up there. I hear she even gave everybody popcorn. That's pretty neat.

I wonder if Mike Graham will go, too. Mike wanted to teach me how to skate and invited me yesterday. That was nice of him. He's one of the few guys who bothers to acknowledge that I exist. But it was lucky I turned him down yesterday. He was skating across the lake like a maniac-- he sometimes acts like that-- and he fell into the water. The rumor spread so fast that he fell in completely and was swimming under the ice. Some guys said he fell in up to his neck, and some said he was totally frozen. It turned out he only fell up to his chest or so. But he got really soaked and chilled and they're a little worried he might get pneumonia.

I went to see him at the infirmary right away when I heard about it, but I didn't want to be obvious. So, I went over to the nurse and showed her the blister on my heel. I've had it for a while, and it had been hurting a lot, but I really wasn't asking for sympathy; I just wanted to see Mike with my own eyes.

I have been having trouble walking on my right foot, though. I think the muscle just tightened up from walking crooked to keep my shoe from rubbing on the blister. Mother and Dad warned me already to have it checked and said I needed to be careful: they said, watch out, it might be my Achilles' heel! They can always cheer me up. So, I did tell them in a letter last night the story of Mike falling in the lake and the latest chapter on my blister, which seemed to grow to supernatural proportions as I wrote about it. I went on and on about the ravishing nurses who soaked my foot in a bath full of bubbles. Honest to God! I know Mother and Dad will get a kick out of it.

Of course, in reality, it was a small plastic trash pail full of disinfectant. My foot does feel better, maybe because I have mostly stayed off it today. Anyway, thanks to my blister, I was able to see Mike. He was lying on a little cot in the corner of the infirmary. I pretended not to notice him while the nurse was checking my foot and getting ready to soak it. After a while, she went into the other room for some disinfectant powder for my heel. I heard Mike call softly to me and I looked over at him. He smiled a shy smile and gave me a little embarrassed wave with his left hand. I went over by his bed. His face was very pale except for two red spots on his cheekbones, almost like a clown's. He must have had some fever. I wanted to take his hand and hold it but I didn't dare.

A really weird feeling suddenly came over me. I remembered the feeling once before when we were in the library. He was there on a couch, dreaming or reading a book and I was watching him out of the corner of my eye. He pretended he didn't know I was watching him but a little smile lingered on his face. Sometimes he acts tough and, sometimes, he has these spurts of wild activity like when he went skating on the dangerous ice, but I know he's more of a dreamer than he lets on, a dreamer just like me.

I knew it then and he must have realized that I was. That's why he smiles that funny smile at me. When he smiles like that, my heart turns over with, I don't know, fear and confusion and a kind of joy I try to hide.

Anyway, I think he likes me and I know I understand him. He wants to prove to the other boys that he is like them, so he acts big and tough once in a while, tries to provoke fights, throws a few punches, but then he reverts back to his normal sweet nature. He tries to fit in and to be part of the in-group. As for me, I've long since given up trying to fit in with the crowd. They used to tease me. Now, they mostly leave me alone and don't bother with me at all. That suits me just fine.

Monday, February 10, 1969

Jeff Hoagland, seeing his friend Larry Larsen in the hallway of their dorm at Andrews Preparatory School called to him.

"Hey, Larry, are you going home this weekend?"

"Yea! Can't wait to get away from here."

"Me too. I'll be going home. It's gonna be great! I won't miss Valentine's Day this year since it's on Friday the 14. I asked to take Friday off and they're letting me. My folks will pick me up Thursday afternoon.

"We'll get a long weekend, three and a half days away from this joint."

"And I'll be able to see my girlfriend and give her a real Valentine in person. You know what I mean? Most of us are getting out of here except for one or two of the real dorks."

"Yeah, that's for sure. Like Rex the Ape, the West Coast geek. He hardly ever even leaves his room and he mopes around all the time. What's the matter with that guy?"

"I dunno. He always has some excuse. He claims he has an awful blister even though he hardly walks anywhere and he never does any sports—well, I guess once in a while he pretends he's playing tennis or ping pong. Like that's a sport. Or then he has a stomachache, and that's because he eats like a pig."

"Hey, have you noticed that lately he seems to be hanging around the infirmary visiting Mike Graham after his stupid dunk in the lake?"

"Yeah, I saw Murray coming out of there just this afternoon. What do you think of those two? Kinda weird, isn't it?"

"It's weird. And they're weird. Still, I would never have figured on those two as a pair. I think we should keep an eye on them. They give me the creeps."

1969. A Summer Day in Seattle

Rex was finally away from boarding school and back at home for the summer.

"Dad, I'm so glad we have a little time together this afternoon. It gives me a chance to talk to you alone. Mother's at the store."

"What is it, Rex?"

"I think you must know by now that I'm not happy at Andrews Prep. School. You know my letters have complained about being on the East Coast, so far from both of you."

"I know, son. And that's hard for us, too. You know we really miss you. But nothing's more important to us than a chance at a first-rate education for you."

"But Dad, I don't like that whole prep school scene. I don't enjoy lacrosse and I'm no good at rowing. I keep on with my tennis but I hate the other sports. As for the academics, I manage ok, but I just kind of feel like I'm just hanging on, even in my French course. I find it hard to speak French with the other students. They sneer because my accent is right!"

"There's something you can thank your mother for!"

"But somehow the grammar and literature are hard. I work at it not to disappoint Mother too much, but I don't really enjoy it. I'm OK in English, I just get by in Math. I do enjoy piano lessons even though I know I'm not super-talented in music."

"The school doesn't push religion on you, does it?"

"Oh, no. We have daily Chapel but no one takes it seriously. When I was younger, I felt kind of comforted. Now, the services just make me more anxious. I feel as though everyone is expecting something from me and I can't do it."

"We've talked about this business of expectations before. You know we don't expect anything from you except that you do your best."

"I know, Dad, but I have been very nervous these past few months. I even picked up a book at the library last week on abnormal psychology and I've read half of it, already. It seems like most of the case studies they quote could have been written about me."

"Now, Son, everybody does that. It's like medical students reading the symptoms of diseases and being sure they have them. It's very common to feel like that."

"I know, but even though I try to remember that, I'm still shocked at how much the descriptions seem like my own personality. I feel like I really am Tom-in-the-closet in Chapter Four."

"Come on, Rex Boy, I know you worry because our family doesn't live a typical middle-class American life. Here you are, your father stuck in his bedroom, flat on his back most of the time. Your mother has to be the breadwinner. At times, I don't even feel like a real man."

"You've always been a great dad!"

"Thanks, son. You just worry too much, Rex. This is the time in your life when you can get a real, top notch education. Do you have any idea how thrilled your mother and I are that you can attend a school like Andrews on a scholarship? You have your whole life in front of you, full of hope, and possibilities. You are your mother's pride and joy. And mine, too. You know, guy, we wanted to meet the plane when you came back to the West Coast in June with Rex Pride and Joy Bishop, the old Ed Sullivan reject team, the American Legion Drums and Bugle Corps, and the 1600-voice Moron Tavern Echo Choir."

"Oh, Dad, you can always make me laugh. You are the greatest. I know I do worry too much, but, honestly, that prep school is not good for me. Really."

"Hold on, son. Do you hear a car in the driveway?"

"Yes, it's Mother. I guess she's back from grocery shopping. Well, that's the end of our talk. But will you talk to her about me and the school?"

"I will, but you'll have to give me a little time. You know how much that school means to your mother. Oh, there you are, dear, our 'bag lady of Fir Grove' is back. Did you bring us all kind of goodies in those paper sacks?"

10

CAROL'S LOVER
Autumn 1979

Harold glanced around the university laboratory one more time. Everything was in order, as he liked it. The racks of test tubes stood against the far wall, sparkling clean, the reference books were back on the shelves. He had glanced at his notes for the next day's class. He didn't need to study them in detail; he knew his subject thoroughly. He could teach this advanced biology class without cracking a book, but he was a conscientious and fastidious professor. He wanted to know that everything was ready for his class the next morning. He could walk out into the twilight with a light heart. He glanced back one last time before closing the door behind him, locking it for the night.

Locking up was both out of habit and out of a sense of responsibility. Some years before, a few biology and chemistry students had made a pipe bomb out of stolen lab compounds, just for fun. It had created only a small explosion and no one was hurt, but he blamed himself for having been careless. Nothing like that had ever happened since, on his own territory; he made sure of it.

Harold had a highly-developed sense of territory and boundaries. His therapist told him it was because he had had to share everything with his four brothers growing up in New Orleans, so now he wanted complete control over his environment at the university. It was true: the only things in his life he could really control had been his work and his classes; he was adamantly loyal to his school for having given him that luxury.

Many professors grumbled about the yoke academia had forced on them, the lack of freedom, the hypocrisy. Harold, on the other hand, felt completely at ease in the university environment.

He liked each group of students he taught, and now he was teaching a second generation. There were the good, the bad, the gifted, the challenged, but he had never given up on any of them. He felt he could impart something that eventually might prove useful to them, even the most rebellious, in spite of themselves. He had found a niche of personal freedom at Meriwether University as a biology professor.

When he was young, Harold had been unable to resist the control exerted by his father, a respected judge, so charming with the ladies, so efficient on the bench and yet such a difficult man at home, especially when he drank too much as he frequently did. Harold was close to his mother and always very protective of her; she was such a Southern Belle, with her coquettish ways and her excessive gentility. When he thought of his childhood, he thought that its hidden darkness could have come straight out of a Southern novel. Of course, when one has grown up in the South, one knows the darkness from within, not merely as a literary device.

He had erased many incidents from his memory but kept deeply hidden and just for himself the Louisiana countryside with its lush landscapes. He knew the pungent smell of the bayous with their green drapery, the geometry of the land with its cypress groves and mossy fronds, the salty inlets near the Gulf, the fragrance of April blossoms, the sharp, fresh scent of newly-caught shrimp tumbling from the net to the accompaniment of the soft splash of water against the hull of the boat, or *bateau* as they used to say.

His wife did not want to hear about those sights and smells; she despised everything Southern. Raised in Eastern Oregon, she believed in the real West and in landscapes of true wilderness. She considered his Louisiana wilderness half-tamed and had little understanding of his world of the Bayou. She had convinced him early in their courting days that the Pacific Northwest was the true paradise. She told of her pioneer ancestors arriving in covered wagons, of miners, farmers and ranchers, tilling and digging and creating, and he found all of it very romantic.

The South came to seem tired and used up, decadent in comparison. One thing good resulted from his transformation to a Westerner. He discarded his bow ties, so he was less the spitting image of his father, though his tongue still purred softly on certain syllables. On tape recordings, he was often struck at how much he sounded like the Old Man.

When he met Pamela in graduate school, she had such energy that Harold could not resist her. He bought her line and swallowed it hook and sinker. That was his most rebellious act against his Southern forebears. Harold and Pamela married, moved to Oregon where he took a position at Meriwether University, and he had been in the Northwest ever since, revisiting the South only for short visits and for his parents' funerals.

Time passed, the children were born, his wife ran his life, or so he thought, never mentioning it aloud. Soon, she refused to listen to any more of his stories. She had other fish to fry and the small fry to raise. Being both a gentleman and a gentleman, he said nothing. Now, he vaguely felt that at some point he should have been stronger or more assertive. When the children went off to college, Pamela still rushed about all the time, to her work, to her book readings, to her walking group, to her volunteer work, to luncheons and dinners with her female friends. She had not cooked a real dinner for him in five years. They even ate Christmas and Easter dinner at the Club since the two children were married with families of their own. Occasionally they flew to visit them in California where both families lived now.

On paper, he had the perfect family, the perfect wife, perfect son and daughter who now had the perfect grandchildren, two on each side: the twin girls and the two boys. He and Pamela could not ask for more. His wife saw her therapist twice a month, one of her girlfriends which always seemed a bit odd to Harold. But in accordance with his wife's advice and with his general policy of keeping the peace, he had been going to 'counseling' alone, once a month.

Strolling along under early evening skies, Harold suddenly came to a decision. "No more shrink for me, ever!" Relieved and elated, he continued his way, pointing out to himself that he did not need help: he was resigned to his mediocre life and the status quo of his relationship with Pamela. At fifty-four, he realized, in the suffused light of sunset that he did not have too much time left. He would refuse to be bogged down by obligations, and counseling was an obligation. Anyway, he had had to think hard to have something to say at what he called 'the monthly séance' with the Freudian-Jungian disciple Pamela had located for him.

Most importantly, there was Carol in his life now. That was the big difference! She listened to what he said and, in turn, he loved the stories she told, even the sad ones about her life. Carol laughed at him, assuring him that she was better than a psychiatrist or a man of the cloth. In her, he felt he had met a kindred spirit. There was not going to be a divorce on his side or hers, but there would be the special moments that they could share, without guilt and in genuine friendship and maturity.

With Carol, he was free to reminisce about his childhood and she would listen when he started to talk about his youth and some events he had nearly forgotten. He was entirely at ease with her and they could cry and laugh together about the quirkiness of it all, their lives included. He was a respected professor and a good teacher, and administrative powers left him alone. He had nothing to prove anymore and had been gently coasting toward a soft exit and retirement, slowly awaiting death.

Carol had changed all that because she was at exactly the same point in her life when they met. She was expecting nothing more from life when they met but was resigned to her situation: a round of professional responsibilities and personal burdens, including a chronically ill husband and a troubled son. Harold and Carol's times together were sacred multicolor moments breaking up the gray dullness of their lives.

Carol loved teaching as much as Harold did. They believed in their educational missions and they could talk for hours about their students and the struggles to educate them. One day, they made a list of the lives they had changed or 'saved,' as they said. Each one could come up with a list of five names they were sure of. They each made a second list of names of 'students touched.' And they could each name eight to twelve of those. They felt very proud of both lists, then a little embarrassed at being so smug, even sentimental, about their saving powers. But they laughed together, agreeing that their professional life had not been just a job, but a real vocation and they certainly could not have been accused of doing it for the money!

Harold liked Carol's story about the young man who had an atrocious French accent, and whom Carol had decided must be discouraged once and for all in his pursuit of foreign language as a major. He had difficulty pronouncing the easiest sounds and could not even imitate correct pronunciations. Though having no facility for spoken language, the young man rose to Carol's challenge, passed all his tests, gradually improved and developed a real love for French literature. He still had a very strong accent but he became a French major in spite of it. He had the fire. In the end, he succeeded in being totally fluent, with a bad accent. A Maurice Chevalier in reverse, Carol laughed!

She told also the story of the young girl who came to her office in tears because she had not turned in a paper on time. By the end of her sobbing, Carol knew the essential facts about the young woman's life. Raised by a single mother, the student had never known her father. She had run away at sixteen and gone to Amsterdam with an American friend. While entangled in the drug scene, she fell in love with a Dutch youth and married him one unfortunate weekend when they were both high. But the boy ended up spending long months in a mental hospital near the capital, committed by his parents. Distraught, the young woman had come back to the U.S., cleaned up her life and had taken her GED. Now she was explaining that she liked college and wanted very much to major in French. But she never could go back to Europe and study in France because she had to pay for her tuition out of her meager earnings as a waitress. She had no money to even think of the travel abroad she would need. Then she sobbed louder, saying that her mother had been a waitress and she could see that she would finish her whole life as a waitress like her mother.

Carol gave her a reprieve for her paper, asked her to develop her ideas for an extra three pages to compensate for the lateness of the work and pointed out to her that each problem should be attacked one at a time. Then, Carol required the young woman to write a diary where she would praise herself for at least one good behavior each day, finishing with the statement, "I love and respect myself."

When four years had passed, the student was divorced, had erased her Holland mistakes, and was at the top of her class. She was able to receive a graduate assistantship as an English instructor in Aix-en-Provence to pursue graduate French studies. She even paid for her mother's ticket to visit her in France. When she returned to the States, she entered a Ph.D. program and never had to return to her life as a waitress.

Walking down the street under the old elm trees with a spring in his step, Harold took a moment to enjoy his surroundings. He loved this old part of town, where much fine old architecture had been preserved. It looked at times like a little piece of San Francisco and liked to think that Portland was at last coming of age as a major West Coast city. Last month, he had rented a tiny studio apartment in the Warwick Plaza, only a few blocks from the university. Carol and he were tired of sneaking in and out of hotel rooms downtown or stealing an embrace behind their office doors at the University. Once, he had been in Carol's office, with the door locked, thank heavens, and a student of Carol's had knocked. They must have made some sort of noise in their secret lovemaking because the student had knocked again saying: "Are you in, Professor Murray? Is someone there?" Afterwards, the two of them were badly shaken, like guilty teenagers caught by the early return of a parent.

They had stayed in the office, not moving for half an hour, then he slipped into the corridor and she left an hour later, still afraid of running into the student. That evening, they met again for dinner and laughed heartily about it, but they knew their behavior was inappropriate and unprofessional. They were falling into the same trap as other illicit lovers.

It was hard to see themselves in that light. He joked again about the cliché of married people having lovers in middle age, and Carol retorted that everyone else was a stereotype, a trite number in the game of life, but when it came to oneself it was always a special case.

"What can anyone say about one's life really?" He inquired, looking at her with a mocking glance, "What would you call your life?"

"Just call it a life; and just call me Carole with an "e."" Carol answered, laughing, her eyes gleaming, her head thrown back against the red plastic upholstery of the booth in the modest Chinese restaurant where soy, garlic, and peanut sauce odors seemed to breathe from the walls.

So, he rented this small place, and no one knew about it, of course. He could afford the apartment without compromising the family budget because of substantial inheritances from his parents, years earlier. Carol and he went to great lengths to hide their relationship, and not a soul suspected they were connected outside the school. At the university, everyone knew they were colleagues and even good friends. They could be seen in the same room at Senate meetings, at Graduate Committee meetings, and on the International Studies Committee. It was easy for them to remain casual in the presence of others because there had existed between them a real friendship for many years before their love affair began.

Walking contentedly in the evening air, Harold made a detour to stop by the local Foodmart. He bought fresh mushrooms, lettuce, new green beans and ripe tomatoes at the store and three roses almost as an afterthought. He had never had much *savoir faire* when it came to courting a woman; his father's womanizing had made him suspicious of any behaviors that could be considered flirtatious or seductive. But as he continued on his way, he smiled at the realization that he was enjoying acting like a spy.

He took a different route every time he and Carol met. For the walk to the apartment he loved to change his appearance slightly. He had a reversible jacket, had bought a French beret which he would put on five minutes before he went through the main door of the Warwick. As it happened, the building was mostly occupied by senior citizens. There was no one from the university here, he was quite sure. A few residents would say hello in the elevator, and he was friendly but distant, usually limiting himself to brief comments about the weather. He kept to himself mostly; other residents probably thought he was visiting an old relative. No spring chicken himself, he did not raise any suspicions.

Today, *en route* to the Warwick, he found himself checking out passing cars, pedestrians and windows overlooking the square, playing at detective for his own pleasure. He wondered if he should grow a mustache; he thought he would ask Carol. He had stocked the kitchen with good wines, pasta, rice and various canned goods, so they could always have supper together if he added some fresh produce. He wished he had found a baguette in the supermarket. Then he would really look like a caricature of a Frenchman with his beret and baguette of bread.

The mustache would definitely help. The image of himself as a Frenchman gave him the idea of bringing his bicycle from home; he remembered that Carol had in her office a poster of a French peasant with bread on the bicycle rack. It was shot from the back, a lonely figure riding peacefully down a long poplar-lined lane. He could store a bicycle at the university, in the laboratory closet. He had the key. Surely no one would recognize him on a bike, with a big jacket and a helmet.

"Well," he thought with a grin, "I could alternate between walking and riding the bike."

Excitement filled his heart. He attributed his current happiness to Carol's presence in his life. He couldn't imagine that he deserved this new chance for happiness at his stage of life, used as he was to thinking of himself as mediocre and insignificant.

Carrying his grocery bag, he entered the lobby of the Warwick Plaza. An elderly resident was advancing toward the door with the help of her walker. Harold greeted her and held the door so that she could maneuver through more easily. The woman thanked him in a girlish voice with the remnant of a Southern drawl, and he wondered if his mother would have turned into a similarly birdlike old lady had she not died of cancer in her late fifties. He was nearly as old as that now. Depressing thought!

He felt grateful once again for Carol's blond wig, her vivacious face and the briskness of her walk. Carol's wigs were famous all over the campus. She looked stylish in them, perfectly put together, and they protected her from the world like a shield. Actually, he preferred her without the artfully waved wigs, her natural blonde-gray hair, feathery, almost straight, surrounding her heart-shaped face. Then, she was her vulnerable self, especially with her head on the pillow looking at him with smiling mouth and sad eyes. What was it between a man and a woman? What was it that remained after the strong animal attraction had waned?

She simply moved him. A biology professor knew of the chemical and biological explanations, but it still puzzled him as a fumbling, tumbling ape-man. He believed the processes of the mind mirrored the processes of nature. But it would have been presumptuous to pretend to understand this parallelism completely. He told Carol that he liked the Greek word "plankton" because that word for the tiny floating fauna on the oceanic expanses really meant 'drifting' and humans were also drifting in certain respects if one looked at their disappointing results through geological time. The complexity of a human's animal body never ceased to amaze him though and he was in awe of its mysteries. He had found in Carol the mystery he could not find in his wife.

His wife was an open book: a direct woman, a true one, a good mother, and an efficient wife. Though fiercely loyal to her invalid husband, Pat, Carol was unapologetic about her and Harold's affair. She remembered her mother's lonely pseudo-widowhood and brought a certain French sense of the right of a healthy woman to the joys of physical love to their relationship. Her unaffected pleasure in bed had been a revelation to Harold, long used to Pamela's reluctance concerning sexual matters.

Carol was passionate, fragile, vulnerable, strong, coquettish, sometimes wavering and sometimes direct. From her childhood, must have come that sense of mysteriousness, lack of solidity, that plankton-ness that he felt in her and recognized also in himself. He could understand it somewhat in himself because of the Southern marshy, mossy lands of his birthplace. But where did it spring from in that Chicago-bred girl? Strangely, he thought of Carol as a girl still, still slightly unformed, malleable, whereas he saw his wife Pamela, the same age as Carol, as a woman, formed, finished.

He turned the key to open the door of the apartment and found himself in their world. The faint smell of Carol's French perfume still floated in the air. He put the bag of groceries on the counter of the tiny kitchen area, and sat on the couch adorned with four soft colorful pillows that Carol had bought. There, the scent of Carol was even more distinct. It set him dreaming.

158

Feet on the coffee table, he closed his eyes. She taught a night class on Tuesdays and Thursdays. She had given herself that slot in order to have an excuse not to go home for dinner two evenings a week, and it worked out well for them. His wife was busy with meetings both nights, and he had long since formed the habit of coming home late. Now he was here, waiting for his love to arrive. She seemed later than usual.

11

THE UNEXPECTED

Carol rushed outside, lifting her face to the evening sky. Free at last. It had been a difficult afternoon with grumbling colleagues who had fought about her decisions from last spring in awarding merit increases. Two years before, she had been so tired of the nitpicking that she had given merit raises across the board, not to slight a single teacher. It went against the grain for her as she believed that everyone should have equal opportunities; but she knew that equal opportunities did not mean equal outcome. This year the Provost had forbidden her to repeat that questionable practice, since clearly not all professors were equal in performance. Carol had done a fair job of assessing all skills, from producing papers and obtaining grants to imparting knowledge to eager young minds, she thought, but now most of the faculty was up in arms, except for the happy few who had been rewarded.

She wrapped her coat closer to her body and tightened her scarf around her neck. The air was fresh but pleasant. It was not raining. She shivered all the same, not from cold but from dismay. Whatever she did, someone was going to complain: always, always there was turmoil. She shrugged her shoulders; she could not wait to reach the apartment and find Harold, to seek solace in his welcoming arms and his understanding of the trials of the academic world. Pat always gave good advice, too, and she would tell him all about the department squabbles in the morning. How fortunate she was to have the loving support of these two wonderful men, each so different but each determinedly supporting her in the battles of her life.

The last rays of sunset were painting the city a soft reddish hue, the tall buildings aglow in the rosy light. Carol made a last effort to shake off her negative mood and stepped into the street. Brakes screeched wildly.

Carol was down in the gutter.

"There was a car accident in front of the Foreign Languages Building." A student cried, looking down into the street from the window of his evening Spanish class. "It looks bad. Oh, no! It's Professor Murray. She was hit."

"Call an ambulance," someone cried.

Carol woke up at the hospital an hour later. Her first thought was for Harold who had been waiting for her in their apartment. There was no phone there, and no way to get in touch with him. Obviously, she could not call his home. She had been lying here unconscious for an hour, while he was expecting her. He must be so worried!

Later she pieced together what had happened with the aid of the nurse and the police report. She had been lucky. The car tossed her in the air and she fell back on the pavement near the gutter. She felt weak and dizzy now as she tried to move each part of her body. Except for a terrible stiffness in her muscles and pain around her neck and head, everything was functioning. She breathed a sigh of relief. She was going to survive with minor damage.

She had a concussion, and someone had called Pat right away. She was to remain in the hospital twenty-four hours for observation. She decided to talk to Rex and Pat over the phone this very minute. They were soon reassured but she firmly refused Rex's suggestion that he visit the hospital.

"Absolutely not. Stay with your father. I'll be home tomorrow. I am fine, darling, really." She cheerfully continued into the receiver. "Do you want to talk to the nurse? Yes, she's right here. She'll tell you. Have a good night's sleep and we'll see each other tomorrow, Rex. You can pick me up. The doctor says I can go home at ten tomorrow morning, so I'll see you then. Here is the nurse. Don't worry; I am fine. Tell Dad he is not to worry. I love you both. Bye."

Later, as the ward darkened for the night, she let herself go. She started crying, then sobbing uncontrollably. She cried for herself, for Harold who would be frantic with worry at her failure to appear when expected, for Pat, unable to rush to her side because of his own diminished physical condition. Finally, she cried for her son Rex, so gentle, so vulnerable, so frail before the harsh realities of the world. She could sense his anguish even over the telephone.

When the nurse returned, she was shocked at Carol's agitated state and gently comforted her. Returning to her station, she obtained the necessary permission and administered a generous dose of tranquilizer. As the medication took effect, Carol's psychological and physical disorientation subsided, and her sobs gradually ceased.

In the meantime, Harold had cooked dinner, and had waited in vain. Somehow, he was not worried. He presumed that Carol had had an unforeseeable delay. When Carol hadn't arrived after an hour, though, becoming concerned, he had walked over to the University and gone up to the Foreign Department. The office was closed as it always was after business hours, but he inquired among some students still in the hallway. By chance one of the students had witnessed the accident and told him what had happened. Calmly, Harold made a few phone calls and discovered where the ambulance had taken Carol. He called a taxi and made his way to Carol's hospital room without hindrance thanks to his air of assurance and his professional demeanor.

Just as she was closing her eyes, Carol heard Harold's calm voice comforting her, felt his cool palm caressing her feverish hand, and she smiled dreamily. A moment later, she felt herself slowly falling away from her surroundings. Numbness overtook her whole being and she slid through an endless cascade of whispering, hushing sounds to reach the silent softness of sleep.

12

REX'S JOURNAL
Tuesday, February 3, 1981

Dad died twelve days ago, on Jan 21,1981. I do not feel any emotion. I have some paranoid thoughts. It is as if my brain is misfiring. I do not seem to be able to concentrate. I have the impression that I should experience some emotional high but that voice inside does not seem to belong to me. Life is confusing and painful. I would like to disappear. I have no desire to do anything. I look at myself from the outside as if in a hallucination and I know I deserve to die.

I have thoughts of suicide. I don't think I have the strength to do it and it would be too devastating to Mother after Dad's death. I HAVE TO REMAIN STRONG FOR MOTHER. Life is so fragile. What a terrible feeling of hopelessness!

13

JUDITH'S LOVER
Late Spring 1938

University was out. Judith was at her aunt's in Minnesota. She had been waiting for the results of her medical test for six long days. Her mind had created threatening projections which had sapped her energy. Her body did not feel it was part of her being. This body of hers, so young and so strong in spite of its petiteness, had served her faithfully for twenty years. She had a lump. A suspicious lump. Could her body suddenly reveal in its recesses an irremediable reality, at twenty-years of age? She was to call the doctor and know the results in the late afternoon, tomorrow.

No one was here to see the feverish glow in her eyes as she waited for the dreaded word which might wipe out her old existence. She'd call tomorrow. One more day's reprieve today.

She decided early this morning that today would be a day unlike any other, whatever the result in the future. First of all, she always disliked her first name. Judith, such an old-sounding name and so biblical! She could use her middle name, Carol. What about Carole with an 'e?' She would think about it. Secondly, she knew that tomorrow and the day after tomorrow she would have to act and react on the medical alert. So, she forced herself to remain lighthearted. She would pretend she did not know anything and that she was going to live forever, with not one iota of change.

In the meantime, this mid-morning, Judith decided to make a quick phone to Lew. He must be working on his family farm. She was delighted to hear that Lew was free, could free himself immediately. He sounded happy that she had suggested an outing, just the two of them. He agreed to everything she suggested, no questions asked. He would come for her right away. They'd have the whole day to themselves.

She dressed carefully, choosing a fresh cotton sundress. She slipped on flat shoes, which she rarely wore. But this was the country, after all. The late spring morning was touched with hues of blue. Trees displayed tiny fresh tufts of pale green at their tips against the backdrop of darker green. New life, new freedom, playing hooky that was what this day was all about.

Lew sped down the highway, easy at the wheel of his pickup truck, Carol at his side, losing herself in insignificant chatter which filled the cab, sending happy threads of inconsequential sound toward him, engulfing him in her warm web. Soon, she stopped talking and slid across the seat toward Lew, touching his arm, his hand, then letting her hand rest on his thigh.

Silence.

The pickup passed long-distance rigs with drivers high above them, elbows resting on the truck window-ledge, eyes checking out those two youths below, more from force of habit and boredom than out of inquisitiveness. The last of the snow had melted a month ago, and the spring day felt almost like summer. Lew took a right turn onto a road which ran parallel to the highway for a short distance before curving away; then right again, onto a deserted road into the woods.

She noticed that the car made right turns only. It didn't really mean anything, of course, but it made her feel as if she were reading omens from the animal entrails or looking for significance in the flights of birds over some agora. No left or 'sinistra' in the landscape. Not for today. Another right turn and the beginning of a gravel road, a rocky dirt road with deep ruts and potholes formed by rough weather and previous vehicles. The wheels met a few slippery puddles where water had collected from the last rainstorm.

Perpendicular to the lane, dried mud had formed large ridges, and the slow-moving truck was jolted repeatedly as it wended its way to the top of the hill. Shrubs and branches scratched the cab on one side, and on the other side the woods dropped away in a steep cliff. He, calm and cool, steered his way through the obstacle course, while she remained silent, slightly frightened, seized by an exhilarating conflict of emotions: happiness, fear and a sense of daring adventure. She felt like that when she was around Lew, especially today. After a difficult maneuver on the narrow path, the pickup stopped unexpectedly, facing the direction from which they had come.

The woods were enveloped in cotton wool stillness when Lew turned off the motor, but soon the chirping of birds started up again. A continuous murmur of cascading water rose in the distance. Slightly slanted sunbeams penetrated the dense foliage and formed iridescent, rosy rays staining the ground in patches of light, like in those Catholic images given to children on their first communion with a saint standing erect, a finger pointed to the sky, his body crowned by a halo of streaking light as if the sun emanated from behind the back of his head. Or perhaps like the heavenly pink sky in the background of a painting from some 17th century Italian School.

She stepped out of the truck, a little dizzy from the rough ride. With a happy, boyish smile, he looked around him, took a blanket, the packed lunch and a backpack from the rear of the pickup. Now he was checking reels from his fishing box and he chose two of them which he placed in the pack along with a flat metal box containing an array of flies.

She carried the fishing rods. Hand in hand, they started down the trail, just wide enough for the two of them.

She felt the warmth of his hand passing through her own fingers, and imagined a tiny minnow gliding downstream or a plump trout riding upstream. Which hand was which? The path narrowed, ending abruptly. He stepped forward and she followed him on a barely visible trail toward the sound of water. Around a turn, the path widened out again and a sheer cliff with two tall, narrow waterfalls rose before them. He turned, let his burden slip to the ground and gathered her in a long embrace.

They stood silent, looking at the line between water and sky, a slight spray floating gently down on their faces. He laughed and his blue eyes changed to match the color of the brook below. Timelessness.

They continued downward toward the stream through thick brush, their backs to the tall trees. Feet sank deep in the soft ground covered with the remains of last fall's leaves.

From a rocky ridge, they could see below the water gurgling over pebbles and boulders. When they reached the stream, he started across first, jumping from rock to rock like a deer; she followed hesitant, and then fell, bottom first, in the river. He grinned at her clumsiness and held out his hand. She was not hurt, not even her pride and she laughed as she shook the water from her skirt. The dress kept clinging to her thighs. They pursued their way, half wading in the river, and half slipping on the rocks. A century-old tree had fallen across the river, forming a bridge to higher ground without the necessity of a detour around the cliff.

"In the woods, balance is what counts." Lew said. She thought she had balance, but she had not counted on the strange environment. She was a city girl. In the woods, she had to think about not being frightened, whereas on the balance beam in gym class, she had no trouble. He held out his hand, now three feet away from her. His assistance restored her confidence and she managed the crossing on the slippery log which was against the far bank at a steep angle. Her skirt was already drying.

As they jumped off the log on the opposite side of the stream, the clearing appeared, a beautiful spot on high ground, dominating the cascading river and surrounded by lofty trees. He was right. It was the perfect spot. He had announced that they would go to the most beautiful spot in Minnesota. And it was true! He spread out their things while she looked around and imagined herself clothed in animal skins like a Cro-Magnon woman in the woods of the Dordogne. She laughed at herself for such trite imaginings.

"This spot is so secluded," she wondered aloud, "how many people have enjoyed it?"

"Not many," Lew responded. "Perhaps some Indians in the old days and a few white men since."

"This would have been a good lookout over the river." She replied, imagining an Indian woman crouched by the fire, a baby in its cradleboard, and, strangely, she felt a deep sense of belonging.

Lew lay down on the blanket he had spread, beckoned to her and she came to sit next to him. He held her in a gentle embrace for a few moments and kissed her tenderly. Then he stood up and took off his clothes. Reclining naked in the clearing, he was as much at ease as in his jeans and tee shirt. That was one of the things she liked about him, the natural way he carried himself, clothed or, now, unclothed.

"Take off your dress; it is still quite damp." He noted and she did as he said.

She had known Lew for years from summer vacations shared as children when she visited her aunt on the farm adjoining his family's place. And she would reconnect with him again every time she came back here. She loved him in many ways but for the first time she could not explain why. What he brought her was a sense of balance between body and mind. She realized there was a raw biological attraction between them, increasing each summer as they'd grown up, and it was all right. But they never had been lovers.

She might be a sex object to him, but so was he to her. They both knew it and they did not need further explanations. For the first time, she was not suppressing her desire, analyzing, weighing, trying to understand. Lew existed just for her in this moment and that was enough. She could now be both vulnerable and living in the present and admit it. That was a big step for her.

He teased her about this new discovery of her vulnerability and about her admitting to it. She had scorned people who wanted to remain in the now. But with him, this day, this one day, she stopped organizing her future. She needed him, wanted him now, even though she could not imagine herself with him ten years from now. He was not part of the continuum she had chosen for her future. It was unwise, naturally. She had an inkling of his shortcomings; he was very much a 'man's man.' But their relationship was not a lifelong love, she was convinced of that. It would last as long as he enjoyed her body and her company, and at the moment that was enough for her, too. She loved him for the fact that he made no demands on her. She made none on him.

Today's decision had changed everything. Every moment he gave her was a gift, and she wanted to give to him too. He was against her now, kissing her more insistently, his tongue between her lips, his hands slipping the straps of her bra down over her smooth young shoulders, then moving over her breasts. She felt a tremor of pleasure sweep through her body, and she pressed close to him with all her desire. She closed her eyes, and then opened them to see his face above her surrounded by the green boughs of the spring trees. She heard the gurgling river, the birds singing, felt the warm breeze brushing their bodies as they came in the clearing, outside, inside, two animals, two human beings, flowing into each other, loving, thinking, not thinking, wanting, coming and becoming. It had hurt just a little for her; she was surprised. And Lew was very surprised that she was a virgin.

Their rapid breathing subsided, after a time, a long time. Tranquility showed in his eyes and was mirrored in her own. she felt in harmony with the entire natural world. Their union, just one among the myriad couplings of springtime was so, well, natural... As they lay relaxed and smiling, a mosquito found his back, and swatting it vigorously, he sprang to his feet to slip on his shirt and jeans over his naked body.

They shared the lunch she had packed, ravenously hungry, and drank the beer that he had set to cool in the stream, tying it to a rope. They drank out of the bottle, taking turns.

"No glasses for us," he laughed. "Aren't we the first man and woman on earth?"

The sun was high in the sky. The clearing was hotter. The breeze had chased the light haze away and the blue sky was reflected in the quiet pools at the water's edge. It was time to fish.

She felt dizzy, from the lovemaking, from the beer, from the mesmerizing sound of the waterfall crashing unceasingly on the pebbles, the hypnotizing sight of the foam rippling back into transparency. She found herself thinking of Debussy and cascades of piano notes, again and again, and then wished she had no such images in her head. She wished only for primitive life, raw associations, the smell of sweat when facing a cougar, the shiver at the sight of a slithering black snake, such as they had seen cross the clearing just a few minutes earlier.

Sitting with her back against a warm rock, she thought lazily of a book she'd read for a history class. The State laws of 1887 quoted prices of pelt. A cougar's pelt fetched two dollars and the scalp of a coyote, fifty cents. Stupid facts amassed through the years, she wished she were not carrying with her. The world of books gave her strength, but it was also a source of weakness. Her emotions were sifted through her learning and at times became fragmented particles. With Lew, she could lose her fact-bound mind and discover the rough nuggets of feelings. She wanted the ore, gold, auricular, aural, oral, not the ring, diamond or wedding band.

He stood on a wide flat boulder in full sunlight, tossing his line with expert hand, the wrist moving an inch forward, snap, pause after a long smooth toss. The yellow line shone in the sun, the long thread glistened, and the furry fly, hardly visible, lay on the water, a tiny floating mosquito, ready to lure the gullible fish. Man's inhumanity to animals, in a Hemingway setting, blue-eyed lover silhouetted against the sky. Was she being caught? She wanted to live an anti-Hemingway story. Was she getting it? What was the blue-eyed lover thinking?

She gingerly climbed down the sloping log and ran to him, jumping from boulder to boulder, wanting his arms around her. Reaching his rock, she slipped and was knee-deep in the torrent for two seconds. Cold waters snapped her into greater consciousness.

"It is not my day for perfect balance." She gasped. And he laughed at her, one eye on the lure and one on her. She stripped and spread her wet clothes around him to dry. Naked, she lay at his feet, every cell soaking in the warmth of the sun, and from below, she watched his wrist, his groin, the buttons on his jeans, his wrist again. "There must be a moral to the story," she thought, with a little smile, "of course, the story of the fly; it's always the same!"

She knew, yet she did not care. For she was happy. Maybe the essential was primitive. Did she get her wish? Could she fall even harder? Man's inhumanity to woman, she questioned, mocking herself.

He fished. She was as if in suspension, at his feet. Her skin absorbed the sun. The warmth of the sun on her pubis made her want him again. He felt it, looked down at her and smiled, muttering something about letting the fish swim a little longer. He lay down on the slanting rock beside her, and soon she was touching him, opening the fly of his jeans, moving her hands to his penis, pulling it gently to her lips. She took his hands and set them on each side. Soon her lips and hands were moving in unison and he came gently, softly, hardly stirring under the burning light of the young afternoon. She kissed him, giving him back some of his sperm, licking his face with long languid strokes of her tongue. Laughing, they slid into the cold water and tumbled in the summer river like two young otters at play, heedless, timeless, mindless.

Later, with the lowering sun on their backs, they climbed the hill, up to the car, up to civilization, up to normalcy, down to the Coca-Cola world. She had had her respite. In the world of the wild, she had almost been able to forget the bonds and boundaries of her ordinary existence, but their reality asserted itself as the sun went down on that remarkable day.

Tomorrow she would have to face the music. For a while she had been able to act as if she were going to live forever.

Would the doctor's diagnosis play havoc with her well-laid plans? That day at the end of May had been a day unlike any other. She drew a deep breath. Now she was ready for the next stop of the train of life.

The next day, she reached for the telephone. She got her answer. Not the dreaded disease she had expected after all. No C word. Just a condition, a benign lump, easily treatable.

What about Lew now?

14

THE SECRET
August 1938

Martha sat in the front room with the letter from Maude on her lap. For a moment, she almost lost consciousness and felt herself falling into bottomless, despairing darkness. With difficulty, she struggled back to the present. Judith, her only child, her shining hope, was pregnant.

When Martha had agreed to Judith's spending summers in Minnesota helping Maude cope with the chores required to feed haying crews, it had never occurred to her to worry about her daughter. Judith was away from the dangers of the city. She was in the healthy air of the country summer. Maude was the liveliest of the three sisters, more adventurous than either Martha or Minnie, but never irresponsible.

Martha had thought that she could feel comfortable that Judith was in Maude's care. She sighed. After all, Judith was twenty years old, hardly a child. It would be unfair to blame Maude for what had occurred.

Martha suddenly realized that in the back of her mind she had feared this possibility ever since Judith started college two years ago, leaving the security of a girls' high school run by strict nuns. When she entered the new stage of her life, entailing more freedom and less supervision, Martha had worried that Judith's ardent nature and love of excitement might lead her into perilous circumstances.

Judith was a conscientious daughter and did not burden her mother with too many confidences, but Martha knew that she went to jazz clubs with her friends, some of whom moved in very liberal, free-thinking circles. Who could say where such connections might lead? Such a lively, pretty girl, vivacious and with such an appetite for life. Any mother would worry about the heedless society of the modern young.

But Martha had been sure of Judith's self-discipline, of her determination to be a credit to the women who had raised her (with only the half-hearted and intermittent participation of a father more soldier of fortune than head of household...) Martha had convinced herself that Judith's aspirations would keep her safe. But, Judith, with all her ambitions, was a modern and independent young woman, which at the age of twenty could result in a certain recklessness.

Martha continued reading the letter, trembling in her hand. The practical Maude had a suggestion for handling Judith's crisis. If the story were to be circulated among Chicago friends and connections that the childless Maude had fallen ill and Judith was staying out of college a year to care for her, Judith would be able to return to school the following year with a minimum of explanation. A great deal of discretion would be required of them all to set up and maintain this fiction, but it would be worth the effort to save Judith's promising academic career and spare the family shame. The fewer people who knew the heart of the secret, the less difficult it would be to sustain the cover story.

Maude wondered whether perhaps Martha might even keep it from Minnie, the third sister, whose apartment in Chicago Judith and Martha had shared for years, but Martha knew that that level of secrecy would be beyond her. She and Minnie had shared the trials of women toiling to hold a household together with too little income and too many strong personalities, and Minnie, herself, loved Judith like the daughter she'd never had. Martha would not have the heart to exclude her from this chapter of Judith's life, difficult though it might be for all of them to bear.

As for the baby, Maude's letter continued, Judith agreed that she was in no position to raise a child, or ask her family to do it. A lawyer and his wife in Holland, a town only a few miles from Pipestone, was known by the local doctor to be looking for a baby to adopt. The doctor a kind, discreet man who would care for Judith, had arranged a few other private adoptions and had assured Maude that the arrangements could be made quietly and with the necessary legal protections for all concerned.

So, there it was. Everything was arranged by the resourceful Maude. Martha felt herself shaken by a storm of complex feelings: jealousy of the confidence and élan with which Maude had always met life's challenges, relief that a way had been found to spare Judith's life lasting damage from this youthful faux pas, profound sadness at the knowledge of the year that lay ahead for her beloved daughter.

A lonely year away from her circle of clever, witty friends. A year away from the challenging studies which she met with such eagerness. Months of experiencing within her the growth of a small life which she would then have to relinquish to the goodwill of strangers, which she would have to mourn in private, which she would never be able to acknowledge publicly.

The sorrow Martha felt for her daughter's situation exhausted her. She dropped the letter on the table and rested her head against the back of the shabby plush armchair for a moment as she considered the loss of her daughter's youth. Then, gathering about her the courage gained from a lifetime of disappointments, she rose wearily and climbed the stairs to explain to Minnie that Judith would not be returning to Chicago in September.

15

CAROL'S SIXTY-THIRD BIRTHDAY
Thursday, May 7, 1981

"Fanny, how kind of you to come. And, oh, you've brought lilacs!"

"I didn't know if Pat's lilacs had bloomed this year. He would have been so happy to see his lilacs bloom."

"They are late in blooming this year. Everything seems late; missing Pat's touch, I guess. I am so glad for your beautiful bunch."

"Rex and you must miss Pat terribly. Well, I also brought you a bottle of Sauternes. Happy birthday, dear Carol."

"Ah, thank you, Fanny. Come in. I used to say that if someone brought me lilacs for my birthday, it would be a good year. I don't have such high hopes anymore."

"Well, nevertheless, we'll hope for a good year. Do you have a couple of glasses for our sweet wine from the country of Graves? No *foie gras* for it, though." They exchanged a small smile.

"Let's sit out on the deck. What a perfect spring evening and the promise of a nice summer. Pat would have loved it."

"Is Rex here? Will he join us?"

"No, He's gone out with a friend, Julie; my friend actually more than Rex's. She's in town. You remember Julie, from last year's picnic in France?

"Of course, how could anyone forget that day! She's not teaching in France this year?"

"No, no. She's back right now, visiting her mother."

"How's Julie doing?"

"Actually, things have worked out nicely for her. You know when I visited her in France, Julie had quite a crush on me and I felt I had to stay aloof with her in order not to encourage her advances. I know it hurt Julie's feelings and I've always blamed myself for not handling things with more sensitivity. But everything turned out all right in the end."

"She did have a crush on you! But what happened?"

"An American girl who'd been living in Spain fell in love with Julie when she visited Agen in the fall and met her there. Both girls are now partners and very happy together. They moved to San Diego when they returned to the States last winter. Julie has a good job with an international advertising firm and her partner is an artist who is beginning to make a real name for herself with her paintings."

"Perfect."

"They've invited me to visit them next summer and I hope to do so. Anyway, Julie wanted to take Rex and me out to a movie for my birthday, but I was glad when you called and gave me an excuse to decline. I don't feel like going out; I sent the two of them off together. We agreed that she'd come over for a visit on Saturday and bring some of her pictures from last summer."

The two women sat for a while in companionable silence looking about them at the May green woods, surrounding Carol's house.

Fanny looked over at her friend, breaking the silence, "Is there anything more beautiful than spring in a Northwest wood?"

"It is beautiful here. I was thinking earlier of Pat saying, many years ago, how few springs we have in a lifetime. He was particularly conscious of it, I suppose, because he lived his life knowing that each spring might be his last."

"And you lived with that, too."

"Yes. You know, lovely as it is, I find spring almost too poignant now. Do you know the poem by Thomas Hardy?"

"No; tell it to me."

"Close up the casement, draw the blind,
Shut out that stealing moon,

She wears too much the guise she wore
Before our lutes were strewn
With years-deep dust..."

"Ah. I see what you mean. The intensity of spring can be nearly too much to bear, at times. You wish for the ripeness of summer or the mellowness of autumn."

"Yes, I look at Julie and her struggles and I look at my poor Rex and I'm ready to sing with Maurice Chevalier: I'm glad I'm not young anymore."

Fanny laughed and filled Carol's glass again, "Listen, we can even hear the breeze in Pat's bamboo."

"And high up in the firs, do you hear the swinging movement of the tree tops? I always think there's such a yearning in that sound, something of the sadness of human life."

"Dear Carol, you must miss Pat so."

"More than I could ever express."

"How is Rex doing? He must miss Pat, too."

"Yes. After Pat's many illnesses I thought we'd be prepared for his death. But all the clichés are true. You really are never prepared for that finality. I think Rex is doing all right. He's still meeting with Dr. Weinstein, the psychiatrist he's seen for many years. It was a blow to Rex, to both of us, really, to find that after he worked so hard to finish that optician course, there are just no jobs."

"I guess it's actually an overcrowded field."

"I don't know why they don't mention that when you are signing up. But we're veterans of the academic business. We know the importance of student numbers; who's going to discourage a possible tuition by pointing out that the professional prospects are grim? Perhaps, let's be frank, Rex is not the best person to succeed at job interviews either."

Carol uttered her last sentence with a mirthless laugh. Fanny was thinking that indeed Rex would be a poor interviewee.

Then Carol called in the silence between them, "Fanny?"

"Sorry, Carol, yes."

"Did I hear you tell Frank that you're going to the Midwestern Modern Language Conference next month?"

"I am planning to."

"And isn't that being held in Minnesota?"

"Yes, I fly into Minneapolis the first weekend in June. It should be a nice trip. I've never seen much of the Midwest and early June is supposed to be pleasant there."

"Oh, yes. I remember Chicago in June. It was one of my favorite months there. I've been thinking and thinking about something. I suppose that since Pat's death in January my mind has been running back over that remarkable time when Pat and I first met, during the war. When we were young and so full of the confidence of our young dreams. Those memories, then my concerns about Rex, took me back to an even earlier time when I was twenty years old. It's a part of my life of which I have never spoken to anyone."

Fanny heard the pain in Carol's voice and turned toward her sympathetically. She was surprised to see tears in the older woman's eyes.

"Carol, *chérie*, what is it?" Fanny reached out and touched her arm, "Is there something you want to tell me? Can I help?"

"Ah, it's an old sad story, but perhaps it's time I shared it."

Carol related the story of the birth of a child so many years ago, in a farm town in southwestern Minnesota. Fanny listened in sympathetic silence to one of the oldest stories of womankind: the life of a young woman disrupted by the unplanned beginning of a new life.

"And now?" Fanny asked.

"That's what I've been pondering. I have no right, I really have no desire even, to meet the woman who was that child of so long ago (more than forty years ago, can you imagine?), but somehow, now with only Rex and me left of this family, and with Pat gone beyond any hurting by this revelation, I find myself needing to know what became of that baby girl. I know the name of the family that adopted her and I know that they lived in a very small town near Pipestone, Minnesota. I think, even in these modern times, family links are more intact in those small Midwestern towns."

"What can I do for you?"

178

"I found myself wondering if you could visit that area and learn something of the outcome of this story. It is clear across the state from Minneapolis, though."

"That's all right. I have Saturday and most of Sunday free before I catch my Sunday evening flight home. It would be easy to rent a car and see a little more of the famous Midwest farm land."

"It might be possible for you to make a few very discreet inquiries. I think it would do me good to know how that baby girl had turned out. The reality might be disappointing. I realize that, but I think I am prepared for that possibility."

"Of course, Carol, you know I will do what I can. Before I go, write down for me everything you know about the family: names, locations, and that sort of thing. I will play detective for a weekend. Are you telling Rex about this?"

"No, no. I am telling no one. No one but you. I thought another woman, especially you, would understand and I know that I can count on your discretion, Fanny."

"Of course, you can! Whose business is it, anyway? I do understand how it could be a comfort to you to know how this daughter's life has gone."

"Daughter. Funny. I have never ever thought of myself as having a daughter. I had spent a careless, thoughtless day, a day like no other, I always thought of it as the fires of youth, I suppose, with a charming young neighbor boy. Ah, that Lew. I can still see those Scandinavian blue eyes! And then when I found myself pregnant. I was of course panicked, distraught."

Did he know?"

"I never told. He knew nothing about it. My Aunt Maude, with whom I had been staying for the summer, who had no children of her own, was absolutely marvelous. She supported me; she worked out a plan that would provide for me, for the baby, and for the family reputation. I missed a year of college, but by saying that I was caring for her during an illness, none of my friends at home in Chicago ever even suspected the truth. Lew had gone back to school by then."

"Then there was the war, I see."

179

"I'm sure it's a situation that today would seem perhaps even grotesque, and with all the openness in today's society, it could not be understood. But for that time, it made it possible for me to continue the life I was just beginning. To my eternal gratitude, it spared my mother and my Aunt Minnie public shame. Not their private grief and disappointment, of course. But to their credit, they never reproached me. We went on the following year as though nothing had happened. I took up my courses again at college and worked harder than ever to make my family proud of my academic progress."

"Did Pat know about this?"

"No, I truly put it out of my consciousness for many years. I think it was the one thing I never told him," Carole said shakily, "Well that, and the fact that I ate steak tartare when he wasn't looking! He knew that I was not completely inexperienced when we were married. He had been quite a lively bachelor himself. We prided ourselves on being modern and accepting new freedoms for women as well as men. I think we both knew that the love between us was of such a different order than anything either of us had ever experienced that those youthful indiscretions were insignificant in comparison."

"Poor Carol!" Fanny reached again to hold Carol's hand.

"Later, when I didn't become pregnant for many years after we were married, and, when, after Rex's birth I had so many complications that I had to have a hysterectomy, I couldn't help wondering if I were being punished. Pat and I had always joked about the large family we would have. Having grown up an only child, without siblings or cousins around, I thought a large family marvelous. Of course, with Pat's health and, to be honest, with my temperament, it's probably just as well a large family didn't work out for us." Carol smiled sadly, pondering the many unrealized hopes of any life near its close.

The two women sat in the deepening twilight, the wistful peeping of frogs in the springtime woods an accompaniment to their thoughts.

16

INQUIRIES
June 1981

Fanny climbed a little stiffly out of her rental car and looked down the Main Street business section of Holland, Minnesota. She had been driving steadily for over four hours and was glad to have reached her destination. Looking around her, she saw a small restaurant, The Main Street Grill. Knowing that she should have had a bite of lunch anyway, she decided to drop in there. It would be as good a place as any to begin her inquiry.

Within a few minutes, she was comfortably seated in a clean booth, with an All-American Burger in front of her. The waitress, a pleasant-faced older woman, came to refill her coffee cup.

Hesitantly, Fanny addressed her, "Would you possibly know of a Hockinson family from around here?"

"Well, there was old Mr. Hockinson, the lawyer. Is that the family you mean?"

"Mm. Yes, I think perhaps so. Carl Hockinson, I believe his name was?"

"Yes, that would be him, Mr. Hockinson. He just died last fall, I'm afraid. His wife, Eliza, still lives in town, mind you. She was the librarian here, but, of course, she's been retired for many years. A very nice, genteel lady."

"And did they have a daughter?"

"Yes, they did. In fact, she and my daughter were in school together. They weren't close friends or anything like that, and I haven't heard anything of Elizabeth in years. She went off to college and she doesn't come home very often. I was always glad my own daughter stayed right here in Holland. I'd hate to have to chase off to California or Arizona or somewhere to visit my grandkids."

The cheerful waitress moved off to wait on three farmers who had come into town for their Saturday shopping and had stopped by for the Grill's famous cherry pie. As Fanny lingered over her own piece of the excellent pie and a third cup of coffee, she heard an exclamation behind her.

Turning her head, she saw the waitress looking out the window, "Isn't it crazy how often that happens! I haven't seen Eliza Hockinson in town on a Saturday afternoon for weeks, but here when we were just talking about her, I look across the street and there she is. Just going into Janice's bookstore over there. Did you see that woman in the blue sweater? That's Eliza."

Fanny paid for her lunch and, thanking the waitress for her assistance, left the restaurant and hurried across the street to the small, untidy bookshop. As she entered, she saw a slender, elderly woman looking through some books on a sale shelf. Moving toward her, she asked softly, "Mrs. Hockinson?"

"Yes?"

"My name is Fanny Taylor. You do not know me at all, but I wonder if I might talk to you for a few minutes. The waitress in the restaurant across the street pointed you out to me. We have, in a way, a mutual friend."

"Yes?" The woman's eyes were reserved but not hostile, and Fanny gained courage for her mission.

"Perhaps I could buy you a cup of tea?"

"Well, Janice has set up a couple of tables there in the back. That would be fine. I'm not in a particular hurry this afternoon. I'm just back on my feet from an early summer cold, and it's pleasant to be out and about again. You say we have a mutual friend?"

Fanny brought a pot of tea over to the table and busied herself pouring out two cups, trying to think how to begin her inquiry. She knew her appearance as a well-dressed professional woman, would help to reassure Mrs. Hockinson. Nevertheless, it was difficult to bring up such an intimate subject with a total stranger. Fanny's innate sense of privacy inhibited her further.

For Carol's sake, however, she persevered, "The waitress, I think her name is Hazel, said that you have a daughter named Elizabeth."

"Oh, Hazel Larson? Yes. Our daughters were in school together."

A small puzzled frown appeared between the older woman's eyes. "Do you know Hazel or Elizabeth?"

"Not exactly." Nothing to do but plunge in. "I have been attending an academic conference in Minneapolis. I teach French at Meriwether University in Oregon. A longtime friend and colleague of mine, Carol Murray, asked me to come to Holland, so I am really here as a favor to her."

"Carol Murray? I don't believe I know that name at all."

"No, probably not. When Carol was a young woman, this would have been in the late 1930's, she used to visit her aunt and uncle in Pipestone. I believe she helped her aunt with cooking and so forth during her summer vacations from college."

Mrs. Hockinson sipped her tea and regarded Fanny with caution over the rim of the cup.

"Mrs. Hockinson, my friend Carol Murray was the young woman, who, in 1939, had a baby which was placed for adoption with the help of a doctor from Pipestone. That baby was your daughter Elizabeth."

Eliza Hockinson set her teacup down with a clink and sat back in her chair, white-faced and speechless.

"Oh, do forgive me. I have given you a shock. My friend has no desire to upset your life or that of your daughter. She is an older woman now and her husband died recently. She has one son of her own, but he has had many difficulties, and she has recently been wondering how the life of her only other child has gone. She doesn't want to enter into your life, or into your daughter's. But she would feel some reassurance if she knew that Elizabeth's life has gone well."

Eliza watched Fanny carefully and took a slow sip from her cooling tea. "I suppose in the back of my mind I always thought something like this might happen. I know that nowadays people are more and more looking for their birthparents and I have always wondered whether Elizabeth might want to do that. But I think out of consideration for me, she has not broached the subject. And really, I had no information to give her."

"I understand."

"One of the conditions of the private adoption was that we have no identifying information about the young mother. We were just assured that all was done legally, that the mother and father were healthy young people, and that there would be no disputes for custody at a later date. As the years passed, we could almost forget that Elizabeth had come to us on the second day of her life rather than on the first. We had been childless for over ten years and were so grateful to have this beautiful baby girl. She seemed like such a gift from heaven, that we felt that to question our fortune in any way would be a kind of ingratitude."

"Elizabeth has never asked about her mother?"

"Oh, I think perhaps once or twice when she was a teenager. But I truly had such limited information that even though I was honest, there was little I could tell her. She accepted that and I could tell that she felt that to push for more information, through Dr. Wohlmann or the like, might only hurt her father and me and she never referred to the situation again. We had always been open about the fact that she was an adopted child."

"Where is Elizabeth now?"

"She lives in San Francisco. She's an art appraiser there and does very well. She has a daughter of her own, our only grandchild, a lovely girl, Caroline. Caroline's a student at the University of California at Berkeley, in fact. They'll be out for a visit later in the summer. They usually come for a week or two just before Caroline goes back to her fall term at school."

"Mrs. Hockinson, I so appreciate your generosity in speaking with me. I know it cannot be easy to speak to a complete stranger about your family, but this will mean so much to Carol."

"Please impress on your friend what a joy Elizabeth has been in our lives. My husband and I never stopped feeling grateful for her presence. The years of watching her grow up, even the difficult time when her marriage to her high school sweetheart ended in divorce some years back, even then we always knew we have been blessed to have her in our lives. And watching Caroline grow up has been equally joyful."

"What a coincidence that your granddaughter's name is Caroline. Is it a family name?"

"No, actually. Mrs. Hockinson gave a little laugh. Elizabeth was a real supporter of John F. Kennedy in her college years and I always suspected that that was why she named her daughter Caroline."

"Ah. Well, Carol will be thrilled to know that a young woman who bears her genes even bears her name."

"And you say she has recently lost her husband?"

"Yes, he died in January. He was a wonderful man. They had a very close marriage and the adjustment has been devastating. I sometimes think that when one partner of a long-married couple dies, it's as though the roots of two old trees have been torn apart. The one that is left, supposedly living, sometimes seems to be damaged almost beyond repair. I hope that that will not be true of my friend Carol, but I'm not sure."

Looking over, Fanny saw that Eliza Hockinson's eyes were filled with tears and realized that Eliza herself has not been widowed long. Impulsively, feeling tears starting in her own eyes, she reached out and touched the other woman's arm. "Forgive me. Hazel Larson told me that you also lost your husband not very long ago."

"Yes. I think the image you used of the intertwined roots is such a good one. I sometimes have felt I could scarcely stand without Carl beside me. But as this spring has come on and I have shaken off the cold I had in the late winter, I've begun to feel that perhaps I will make it, after all." She smiled a small brave smile and asked, "So now, Mrs. Taylor, what would you have me do?"

"Oh, nothing, Mrs. Hockinson. There's nothing to do. I will give you my card. Here. Should any question arise, medical or something like that, if you should have a need to contact Mrs. Murray, I would ask that you do it through me."

"I might not."

"You don't have to. Carol is not very strong right now and it would be better for me to relay any questions or information for her. I don't think she will contact you again. I can assure you that she would never try to contact your daughter or your granddaughter for that matter, without letting you know. She is a very discreet person." Fanny smiled, "She's French, you know."

Fanny paid for the tea, bid farewell to the older woman left alone at the small table, and returned to her rental car to begin the long drive back to Minneapolis.

Her spirit was heavy with the day's dealings in secrets shared and unshared, secrets kept and secrets revealed.

17

REX'S JOURNAL
Sunday, January 24th, 1982

Dad passed away a year and three days ago. It is the anniversary of his burial today. Now, I can remember what Father was really like, what he read, what dishes Mother cooked for him, what he said to me and what Mother said, what the two of them talked about through the years. A year ago, I could not remember anything.

I feel like I'm coming out of the deep dark hole I have been in since Dad died. I have not cried since, though. My eyes feel as if there are no tears in them at all. But at least, I can get out of bed and eat my breakfast without feeling like throwing up. I definitely am better than last year because I see now that Mother needs me, so I am here for her.

It seems to me I am replacing Father in some way. She goes to work regularly and appears to enjoy her routine again. She's got lots to worry about with university matters but she has regained some of her old determination, outwardly at least.

She rarely smiles but she doesn't cry all the time, either. I wonder if she is still taking those sleeping pills. The doctor gave me another month's supply of mine, thank God.

I try to be strong like her and for her.

1984, Saturday, July 28

During the day, I am fine, but I watch TV till the wee hours of the night, and dark thoughts assail me. It is then that bits and pieces of dialogue come back to my mind; it's Mother's voice. I hear her say to me: "Do you remember when your father planted these bamboo trees in the garden? You were only ten years old."

Daddy's gone and the bamboos thrive. Why do trees survive the people we love? I remember when Dad talked about his best friend who had fought in France during the war, an Army Intelligence officer. That man loved two types of trees: the palm tree and the mimosa tree. Apparently, his own father had planted a palm tree in the garden at his birth. So, when he was older, he always took great care of "his" tree growing in the middle of the lawn.

The year his father died the tree froze because of a rigorous winter. The son would say it was right that the tree and the man who had planted it died at the same time. And the mimosa tree died, too when he, the son, in turn passed away. There was something that seemed right about those men's deaths and those of the trees they loved. But those are exceptional cases.

For most of us, our trees outlive us, and that's the true way of nature. The bamboo trees thrive and I still mourn my father's passing.

18

CAROLINE'S ARRIVAL
Wednesday, October 22, 1986

Caroline felt a rush of exhilaration as she sped north on the I-5 freeway. She should be studying but she was driving instead. She loved long drives, and this ride up the highway was going to be nice and long. The whole idea had a soothing effect on her mind. She did not think about anything in particular and was relaxed behind the wheel of her small Japanese car.

Having taken a few days off from her term at Berkeley Graduate School, she felt free to go to Portland, as free as the autumn breeze blowing through the Siskiyou Mountains. Caroline's curiosity and sense of adventure were pushing her north to try to close the loop of her biological history.

She realized that her mother might have felt more of a sense of urgency had she been in Caroline's place. But for Caroline a sense of calm, even contentment, was dominant. Her adoptive grandmother, the Minnesota woman who with her husband, now dead, had adopted Caroline's mother and whom Caroline adored, had passed on to Caroline all the information she had received from a Fanny Taylor.

A person named Carol Murray, her mother's biological mother, had just died and the funeral was two days from now. Mrs. Murray's son, Rex, was the only known remaining relative. Fanny Taylor hinted that it would be better for Caroline not to see him, as he was unaware of his mother's past. The only persons who knew anything about this chapter of Carol's life were Fanny Taylor herself and a Harold Townsend, both longtime friends of Carol Murray.

Caroline had set her mind on attending the funeral of this woman she did not know but to whom she owed her very existence. Moreover, from her grandmother, she had the addresses of those two strangers, Fanny and Harold, who could help her fill in a gap in her own history.

She did not feel much saddened by this death. After all, she had never seen the woman, and her "real" grandmother was the one she had known since she was an infant. Many adoptees have a compulsion to discover where they came from, and they search determinedly for their lost relatives, but her mother had not been like that. Caroline herself felt a certain curiosity, but not a profound need for an extra emotional bond. She was determined not to appear disloyal to the couple who had sacrificed so much to raise her own mother.

But having discussed the situation with both her mother and her grandmother, she could attend the funeral with their blessings. Her hope was to learn some useful facts to report to her mother, and there was no disloyalty involved now that death had ended all competition. Since Caroline had been told the truth from the beginning, there was not a single discrepancy to be explained.

Her deep blue eyes, for example, could have been surprising with her brown-eyed mother and green-eyed father, but one grandmother had gray eyes and her grandfather blue eyes. How did the Laws of Mendel work again? She shrugged her shoulders. As for those biological facts, she did not bother very much about genetic codes and inherited factors from one unknown biological grandmother. In her down to earth approach to life, she was who she was, with wit and intelligence. She was not vain or egotistical. Caroline considered herself a well-balanced person. She enjoyed sports and the outdoors; she was comfortable in her own body and most people found her pretty. For all that she felt lucky and grateful to the relatives she knew and also to the young woman who had placed her mother for adoption ages ago, eons earlier, in fact, forty-seven years ago, in 1939!

She could hardly understand emotionally a time when a woman was a slave to her biology. Caroline believed every door was open to her: she could have a career, she could decide when to have a baby, and even raise it alone if she decided to. She did not plan to do that, however, because she was confident that she would choose a perfect husband and a perfect father for any future baby.

She believed in love, if not love at first sight. Her whole life lay in front of her.

She pressed the knob of her car radio and a Glen Miller tune filled the car. She loved it, saw it as a premonitory sign, and tapped the steering wheel in time with the swing rhythm. She wondered if her biological grandmother, now dead, had danced to this music. She must have, she said almost aloud, musing, and Caroline had a flash in her mind's eye of a petite woman, young and lively, dancing with an energetic blue-eyed farmer's son from Minnesota. It was an image of great *joie de vivre*. In an instant, it was replaced by the image of her mother's own figure as a young fiancée dancing to the Beatles. Weird, she thought as her own silhouette superimposed itself on that of her mother's. Caroline herself grew up with the Beatles. Was it the first time two generations had enjoyed the same pop songs?

Music is linked to the events of our lives more than we realize, she reflected. She saw herself learning to dance at Middle School dances, and laughed out loud at several other music-filled memories of her childhood, already so far away. She had led a fortunate life and hoped that it would continue. She remembered her first crush in high school and how much in love she had been with Chris Snyder. "What did I see in him?" She wondered. Her laughter rose again into the October sky as she crossed the border into Oregon.

Caroline stopped for gas and then concentrated on her driving as she pulled back onto the freeway, her mind totally absorbed by the gray ribbon of road unwinding steadily in front of her. When she saw the signs for Eugene, she breathed a sigh of relief. She was in a place she knew. She loved the open road but received comfort, too, from familiar spots.

She had visited the campus two years before to see a girlfriend who was studying at the University of Oregon. Caroline considered stopping there for the night, but it was not late, so she decided to keep driving north. Brownsville, Albany and Salem were just green signs with pointing arrows on the freeway. It was only when she saw the sign for Highway 99W that she stopped again for a cup of coffee at a truck stop. She recollected that her Eugene girlfriend had told her how pretty the Willamette Valley looked in the fall and how the Oregon wineries would one day compete with California's. She had teased her girlfriend, originally from the Midwest, about her enthusiasm as a transplanted Oregonian and a wine connoisseur.

Then Caroline remembered that while Fanny Taylor, who had called her grandmother in Minnesota, lived in downtown Portland, Harold Townsend, the other old friend whose name and address her grandmother had given her, lived in Dundee. He and his wife had retired in Oregon, buying an old Victorian house that they had restored to its original splendor. She was in Oregon, on 99W and their house must be only a few miles from where she sat in the café booth. The truck-stop waitress was friendly, glad to give her directions. She even suggested a bed and breakfast in Dundee where Caroline might spend the night after her long day's drive.

Caroline felt her luck holding when she reached the small vineyard town an hour later and checked an address in the telephone book retrieved from the bottom of her purse. She was delighted to stop in front of a dignified Victorian house with a long porch where enormous jars of chrysanthemums spilled over with splashes of fall color. She could catch a glimpse of a rolling lawn behind the house. Mr. Harold Townsend must live here and he must be an excellent gardener, she surmised.

Her heart was beating fast as she lifted the knocker which was in the shape of a lion's head and which reminded her of the arms of Florence and the many handsome doors she had admired in Italy. Facing the closed door, she imagined she was back in Italy where she had spent her junior year abroad. She was glad she had chosen to do as little studying as possible, just enough to earn decent grades and she had packed in a lot of traveling throughout Europe.

Now a man was standing at the door. "Yes, Miss, may I help you?"

She noticed the sad eyes in spite of his polite smile. His head reminded her of the brass lion on his door: big mane of whitish hair, golden eyes and strong teeth. He was not a handsome man but striking. He exuded a certain old-fashioned charm, his style a little remote, in spite or perhaps because of his age and impeccable manners. He studied her face for a long time to the point where she began to feel slightly uncomfortable. His sad eyes opened wider as he studied her features.

"My God, you must be Carol's granddaughter," he exclaimed. "I can see her in you. She must have looked just like you at that age."

Suddenly shy, Caroline didn't confirm her identity right away, standing on the porch with an odd lump in her throat in front of this older gentleman with trembling hands and glistening eyes, overcome by intense emotion.

"You know that Carol is being buried tomorrow." He murmured, recovering some of his composure.

"I'm driving up for the funeral." She replied in a voice as shaky as his, his emotion having been transferred to her as if by osmosis.

"Forgive me for keeping you standing outside. Please, do come in. Carol would have been so happy to know you. I still remember the rainy afternoon not long after her husband's death when she told me about your mother's birth. I was honored by the confidence as I think no one else knows except Carol's French friend, Fanny Taylor."

After real introductions, they sat in the living room and he busied himself opening a bottle of pinot noir from the Dundee area. When they took little sips of their wine, he went on talking about Carol. "There always existed a special corner in Carol's heart reserved just for your mother. And in her later years, it was a comfort to her to know that a part of her lived on in another woman."

Two hours passed. Stories were told, photo albums were opened, lives unfolded. Harold grew animated and told of his long friendship with Carol and his role as her special confidant. He dared reveal to Caroline, now a kind of instantaneous surrogate granddaughter, that he was bereft because of his deep attachment to Carol. He felt that he was somehow being punished by fate because he had lost his wife the previous year and had suffered another loss with his dear Carol's death. He was profoundly grief-stricken and found that he was mourning both women together.

"I loved them both and, yes, it is possible to feel deeply for two women simultaneously. I am the living proof of that fact." Harold concluded staring in Caroline's eyes.

Caroline was moved by his candor and the dignity of his suffering. She could feel his loneliness in her own bones. She, who had thought that part of her mother's past had little significance only a little while earlier, gradually felt great tenderness toward this aging stranger who had loved her grandmother. One's heart could always expand to include another love, and in those two magic hours her heart accepted two more human beings: the recently deceased Carol and the living but lonely Harold.

"I haven't had any dinner, let's have supper together." Harold suggested. So, they went out to the little French restaurant he knew that had an excellent table.

Coming back to his house, he offered her the guestroom and she accepted in all simplicity.

After all they were going to the same place the next day, Carol's funeral. They would take her car to go there. He was relieved that Caroline would do the driving. He was getting nervous when he had to drive a certain distance.

"Age…" He sighed.

19

THE FUNERAL
Autumn 1986

I am immobile in my coffin, I, Judith Carol Jensen Murray, born May 7th, 1918, in Chicago, Illinois, deceased October 23rd, 1986, in Portland, Oregon.

It has already been six days since I passed away.

I am only sixty-eight years old. I look good for my age. People tell me that I appear ten years younger than I really am and I pretend to believe them. I am a little vain and I do not publicize the number of my spring times. By the same token, I do not hide them either. If I were asked, or age was alluded to, in a proud, forceful tone I would tell my age to the exact day. I suppose I should be talking of my wintertime now, or my "third age" as the French would say. As for Shakespeare, the Master would certainly allude to the seventh and last act of life's drama.

"Spring!" What a beautiful word. After all, I was born in the spring, in the month of Mary, the Virgin. I will have my way just a little longer, and will not speak of Doom's Day or May Days but of real springs, fountains of youth, waterfalls in a Japanese garden and whispering bamboo fronds caressing the water lilies of the pond.

It's fitting also to say good-bye in the fall, at the end of October, my favorite autumn month. The foliage changes. Reds and browns rival with yellows and golds and make the Northwest look almost like Vermont. Some believe that non-deciduous trees do not drop their leaves. Well, they do not live in a real wood filled with firs and cedars. Evergreen trees do shed their needles, but gradually, never at once. In my experience, they shed all the time, constantly, in all seasons so we don't notice, but, in my garden, I do notice.

Perhaps that is my little hellish punishment in life, just like the water pouring out of the broken cistern of the Danaids, my little plight on earth. I did not have to empty the water or roll a rock up the hill like Sisyphus. I had to sweep eternally, in my lifetime, at least, those damn pine needles. Trust me, I could have swept the terrace morning and night to get rid of all the fine rust-brown pine "evil things" accumulating on the terrace. I do, or rather I did, the sweeping every other day, and only if Rex had not done it himself, first. Sweeping pine needles till I dropped dead, that was my purgatory. What a fate in Hades! I hope with all my heart to have a more exciting task than that now.

Sixty-eight years old.

"It's still too young to die," murmurs one of my colleagues from the university, one of my generation, waiting in the lobby of the funeral parlor. The guests are slowly entering the funeral chapel for the service. These are my cherished, loyal colleagues, those on my side, I mean. They stand together, same ideals, same generation. These people fought with me, stood by me, and gave me a little sunshine during my days at work. The younger university and high school profs whom I have loved and nurtured through the years stand in a little group over to the right, saying nothing. They think that I am lucky to have lived to such a ripe old age. They do not realize how fast life goes, much faster than one expects.

I remember being a young bride, then a mother and all of a sudden, here I am, I could be someone's grandmother. That is when I realize I am lucky. I have known the love of a family, husband and son. I have had a career; it was not so common for a woman of my generation to teach at a university, even if not the first top ten ones. Still I consider myself a failure. I did not live my life to the fullest. I had ideas of grandeur when I was young, hopes to become famous in the intellectual arena. I admit it now. There's nothing more at stake, nothing to lose.

I knew I was bright, and I have not done the best I could with my wits and my gray matter. But it is too late to complain, and when I think of the choices I had, I realize I would make the same decisions again, I would not have acted differently. I never had remorse or regrets during my life; I am not going to start now!

If those young folks knew what I know, they probably would not work, would not do anything. I sound just like my mother. Eventually, we turn out to be more like our mothers than we expected. And I fought so hard to have a different fate than my mother. Looking back, she may actually have been a happier person than I. No regrets, dear. Chin up. Everything comes back to one's point of view.

My point of view, this very second, is interesting. All the 'alive' people look taller! To live one's burial was a nightmare of my youth; or a dream. I say a dream, because even then I considered it with a calm and peaceful state of mind. And I was right. For here I am, looking beautiful, feeling entirely at peace. Let me rephrase that. Not entirely at peace, or it could not be me. May I say passionately calm, or divinely peaceful, but still feeling the fire of joy within me? With a desire to fight, fight what?

Fanny, my French colleague, with the help of Julie, a student from younger days, organized this service. They have done a good job. It is thanks to their love and energy that the ceremony is going well, for Rex is totally distraught and would have been unable to cope with these arrangements.

Poor son of mine. Fanny went home with him yesterday to choose my finery to wear. Anyway, why did I imagine my burial when I was young? Primal scenes always attracted me: birth, death, and love in between those two poles, if one has luck enough to love and be loved. It was a little morbid for me to think of my death when I was so young. But now I can measure what I imagined as a child against the here and now. Somehow, it seems less romantic than in my fanciful childhood beyond-the-grave experience. Why did I think of dying? Was it a way to verify who would cry at my funeral? Was it good for my ego?

Other dreams inhabited my psyche: the falling dream, the flying dream, the dream of the big wave that rolled ashore and engulfed me, but never quite succeeded in overcoming me, and the grain of sand in the desert that grew into a huge ball and tried to catch me, and never did either. Freud talks about those dreams, of course. Most of them he finds sexual. I disagree, partly.

LET IT BE. May I rest in peace with Freud, but not too close. I would rather be on the side of his patient, Dora, or even poor Madame Freud. Back to the funeral dream. Perhaps it is to discover if we were right about the people who do not like us. We can discover if our intuition is correct? Or, instead, surprise, astonishment that people who counted in our lives did not make the effort to be present at the memorial service. Feeling too sad to come? Perhaps just too fearful to confront death, too busy with their everyday lives, too absorbed to alter or complicate their routine, too finicky to find the perfect baby-sitter or whatever? Life always gets in the way of death. Life always prevents someone from uttering the last good-bye.

Then someone we haven't seen for years does indeed show up. Positive vibrations. Indeed. Here is Trudy. She seems really shaken. She came up early, before everyone else and asked to see me. She looked at me in the coffin. And she did not recognize her old friend, me! I could hear her thoughts:

The person lying in this coffin does not look like Carol. Time was kind to Carol before, but now this is not she. She has such beautiful facial contours still, but nothing else I can recognize. The vacant expression. Poor soul. I feel guilty for having lost contact with her. I remember when we were both practice teachers in Chicago in 1942. Then she got married and later I helped her and Pat move to Oregon. We were close then. They stayed at my parents' home before they found a house of their own. Carol always lived on the south side, and I lived on the north side of town. North and South, different lives, different styles. Mainly, we were both busy people, so our visits lessened. Carol and I got together now and then, but we saw less and less of each other. Then my family, husband, children and all, went to New York for two years.

We returned to the Northwest later, but for the past several years Carol and I were completely out of touch. One day not long before she died, Carol called me out of the blue. I was thrilled to hear from her. We chatted over the phone like two schoolgirls recalling old times. It was delightful. I suggested we make a date to have lunch but Carol refused, without explanation. This puzzled me. Pat had died over five years before. When I asked about Rex, she said he had gone through a nervous breakdown. Carol was very reluctant to talk about her present life. She did not sound like the "old Carol" I knew.

I wondered why she had called if she wouldn't see me. Being here for her service makes me understand. I feel terrible, in fact. I realize now that she reached out to me and I did not recognize her call for help. Now, I can recall the tone of quiet desperation, understand the long pauses, understand her joy when we evoked the good times of our youth. She even asked what happened to Joe Brandt, whom she dumped for poor Pat. And asked about Lew. I had not thought of him for such a long time... Forgive me Carol, for not being the friend I should have been. I should have heard the cry for help in your silences. But dear friend, I had never seen you depressed. You had your serious side, but we could always count on you to lighten our spirits. I never imagined that you could have needed your spirits lifted by me, the one who tended to stumble along, doing the best she could. Forgive me, my friend of old.

What Trudy is thinking is accurate. I, Carol, Judith as she used to call me when we were young, can attest to it. Here she is sobbing from the bottom of her heart. You are completely forgiven, dear Trudy; there is nothing to forgive. How did it go? It's hard to remember the last few days; it's too recent. So many strange thoughts overtook me. Yes, I remember. I did call you a week before my passing to the other side. I did not want to go to lunch, of course. I already looked a mess by then. Rex hardly left my side.

I made a few phone calls to the people I cared for, when Rex was picking up some groceries at the corner store. I called friends as if I were a thief, hiding from my own son. What a pity! I called Trudy, and Mary Maloney back in Chicago, bless her big Irish heart. She could make me laugh even at the end. Though I didn't admit it, the calls were my way of saying good-bye. I knew I was going to go. And I called Kimberley too; she is my too straight-lace friend, the English teacher, with whom I went to London in 1958. One always knows deep inside it is time to go. I tried hard to hide it from Rex. Towards the end, he had almost become my double or perhaps my half, who knows, poor child of mine.

To die on a Thursday morning! What an irony. The irony is apparent to no one but me. For me, in my life, Thursday had always had a special meaning. It is hello, beautiful day. *Bonjour*, sky; *bonjour*, sun. Hello, earth! Hello, the whole France. I think my grandmother was the one who taught me that *jeudi*, Thursday was a special day. I loved my grandmother, better than my mother in a way, because she had time to take care of me. And we had the French language to the both of us, alone. Whereas my mother always worked, always complained, resented my father who had deserted her to go to Spokane to be a lumberjack, a 'jack of all trades with lots of Jills,' she called him, at times; and once or twice even a 'jackass.'

My grandmother's stories were wonderful. She came to this country when she was still young, but she had started her schooling in a country school in the South of France. The schoolhouse was next to the church. The schoolmaster played cards with the priest, and they argued forever over the merits of a religious education versus a lay education. My grandmother's house was on a hill, and she had to walk three kilometers to school. It sounds just like the stories old folks like to tell. When *Mamie* lived in France as a little girl, most peasants never went to school; but she was the first who could read in her family. It was the time when the French Government started to apply the rule of "Separation of Church and State." The new law took elementary education out of the hands of the Church and put it into the hands of State teachers, rendering education compulsory for all, including girls. Within a year, she could read to her father the week-old newspaper that the priest used to give her after catechism, on Thursday morning. On Thursday, that special day, there was no school, you had fun and were excused from farm chores. The morning was reserved for religious education and the afternoon for games.

Grandmother's father had befriended an old lady who did not have the strength to attend to her garden. He took care of the old lady's garden all of Thursday in exchange for music lessons for his daughter. *Mamie* would go to Ermine Magnan's beautiful house in the village and hear her father work in the garden while she learned her do, re, mi, fa, so, la, si, do. Every Thursday, she would look forward to her catechism in the morning and piano lessons in the afternoon. Without hurrying, she carried the piano book loaned to her by Madame Magnan who had painstakingly drawn the two middle octaves of the keyboard on a piece of cardboard for her to practice at home. Of course, her parents did not own a piano.

In Chicago, *Mamie* told me all the stories of her childhood, each year of her youth corresponding with events of my life at the same age. At times, her life seemed to have been mine. Was it she or was it I walking unhurriedly down the hill, piano books under the arm, sauntering half the time in the shade and half the time in full sunshine, crossing straight through the fields, but making zigzags as soon as she or I entered the village? The piano teacher would hit the edge of the piano with her pencil at times, whereas the schoolteacher made you do the 'rosebud' with your hand if you did not behave. You would have to hold your fingers up together and offer them to him and he would hit the tip of your fingers with a ruler when you did not know your numbers or multiplication tables. *Mamie* went in the corner only once, and she had to wear the donkey's hat, a kind of dunce cap with long donkey's ears. She was mortified and always studied her lessons after that so that she would never have to return to the corner.

She had a favorite fairy tale that went with the story of the dunce cap. It was the story of 'Donkey Skin' where the princess had to hide from her father not to be forced to marry. What I remember best were the three dresses of the princess: the dress 'the color of the sky,' was as blue as heaven; the dress 'the color of the moon,' was silver, dusted with stars; and the third dress was as bright as the sun and made of gold threads and diamonds. *Mamie* enlarged my dreams with those beautiful dresses worn by the poor swine-tending girl in the secret of her hovel.

Think of it! *Mamie* herself when she died was younger than I am now, lying motionless in the funeral chapel. She seemed so ancient to me, then. In life, her hands were always doing something. They fascinated me. Especially when she was tatting. She had an ivory netting-needle given to her by Madame Magnan, her piano teacher, that she kept all her life. All farm women were adept at knitting or weaving, but tatting was more of a bourgeois pastime. My grandmother tatted with such speed that I could not see what she was doing. I could only perceive two larger birds flying full speed around a tiny ivory one. Those birds were so active that the whole house, the neighborhood and friends' houses were replete with doilies. By the time I was ten years old, my trousseau was comprised of five doily tea sets, two tablecloths with tatted edging, and a dozen decorative doilies for vases and knick-knacks.

Isn't it just like Rex to have remembered his great-grandmother's stories, from my own retellings? The silk pillow holding my head at this very moment is decorated with one of my grandmother's ecru doilies. Thank you, Rex, for remembering. You are a sensitive man, in many ways a child in a grown-up body, too fragile for the harsh modern world. You did not think of my clothes but you remembered the doily.

Thursdays had a meaning in my universe as it did in my grandmother's. It was a filled ball, a rolling ball, a loving dancing ball, and a whole world in one as described in the British poem written by Marvell. Isn't it marvelous to be called Andrew Marvell? I had particular feelings for every day of the week: Monday was the dull one; Tuesday, the serious one; Wednesday picked up some charm; and Thursday was the superb iridescent ball, the world rolled into one. Friday remained a fair-weather friend; Saturday was the day we took a bath. I shower every day nowadays, but I still take a weekly bath on the weekend, that is, I did, up until last week.

That Thursday, October 23rd, the ball developed a leak; the blimp deflated; the balloon was punctured; the goldbeater's skin turned out to be tin. The pigskin, ox intestine, wild boar leather, all are no good. The skin sinks, the flesh is weak. Motionlessness of my features. My jaw icily set beneath the pink make-up. The mortician claims to be an artist. I am the first to admit it. I look beautiful, they all say. I don't recognize myself. Blood red lipstick, heavy mascara, pinkish-beige foundation. Too much rouge on my cheekbones, which are high and good. I hate makeup now. It looks unnatural when you are alive but more natural when you are dead. How strange! They made sure I wore my best BLONDE WIG. I suppose it looks like me, after all.

It's strange to be here lying on my back in front of everybody. One usually lies down in private. The lying down position was a way of life for Pat, but I was a woman on her feet: running, rushing, the epitome of movement. Lying down was not my favorite state. Although I do have wonderful memories of times when I found myself with my head on a pillow. With Pat, my true love, I shared great moments. It was during the war. Everything was felt with more intensity and more urgency in 1943: a date, a dinner, a sudden engagement, and joyous lovemaking all in a few short hours. I was caught by surprise by the sheer power of my desire for Pat, and his for me. One weekend decided our fate for the next half century. What an extraordinarily happy couple we made!

I always wondered about Pat's kidney disease. Did he get it when he was in the Army Intelligence? Was it because of some kind of weird poisoning? He complained of his tonsils that they took out, of his arthritis that they treated, but his kidneys? He never talked of his involvement at the time, but I was sure he worked for FDR. Why did Pat disappear for two weeks at the time FDR was in Tehran, Iran at the end of '43? Well, I'll never know. After the early years with Pat, when his ill health left him so debilitated, I have to confess to a lot of flirting with other men. It gave me the illusion of still having a sexual life. Poor Pat.

I take the responsibility of one real affair in my lifetime. Come, Carol, tell the truth now, two real love affairs, really: one before Pat, one after Pat. Three men in my whole life. For the first love, I never, never, talk about him. Lew was a good young man, I liked him, desired him. Pat, my husband, is my everything: he is Janus, the other side of myself.

The third man, Harold, meant a lot to me because of his kindness. He is coming in now, entering the hall of the funeral chapel. I see him opening the door, walking in slowly. He looks grief-stricken. Thank you, Harold. Thank you for the time we shared. You were a friend who gave me all the support you could, a shoulder to cry on; you showed me I still was a desirable, not-so-old woman, not a man-hater, old-maid, absent-minded professor, at a time when I was disliked, perhaps hated, by some of the frustrated, aggressive male professors I had to work with. I shiver just thinking about all that again.

A young woman with blue eyes is entering just after him. Who is she?

My son shivers also. His big body of a man trembles. He looks like a tortoise without a shell. I was his shell. What will become of him? I should have had more strength to protect him. Fanny told me I protected him too much. There's some truth to that. But I could not protect him from important dangers, thus I failed him. At thirty-five, or is it thirty-seven, time goes so fast, he might still find a nice girl who could take care of him. He even could have a child. Our name, our line would not die after him. I have to keep this positive thought in mind. But I doubt it. I always suspected he had homosexual tendencies.

I have to learn to let go of my son once and for all. We were so happy, Pat and I, when I became pregnant, and we hoped to have several children; I had always found the life of an only child lonely. But Pat was never very well again. There were complications with my own body, so that no other children could follow. Rex was our conqueror, our hope, our future, our claim on eternity. Forgive us, Rex: I never foresaw the deluge of catastrophes that ensued.

Your father, my husband, bedridden as he was for so long, caused by his secret, hidden, dangerous job during the war, of course I guessed some - we won't talk about it, it has to remain secret for Pat's sake - offered us the stable and quiet raft that we needed among the tumultuous white waters of life. Though sickly, he was good to his country, good to us and good for us. He stood, or sat up in his bed, but still he stood by me, always, for thirty-eight years.

He towered over you, my son, for thirty years of your life. You inherited his big frame and large shoulders and you took after me in the eyes, deep and serious, and the little turned-up nose. That somewhat tilted-upward nose gave you an air of innocence, a *je ne sais quoi* unusual in your wide man's face, whereas it gave my woman's face a cute and cheerful air, compensating for, distracting from the sadness of my gaze.

I remember you, Rex, at five, admiring the lines of ants working away at their chores. You could not believe they would go up a blade of grass one way and descend the other way, without varying, because the leader had chosen that route. You were so smart, you already knew the straight line was the shortest path between two points. One morning, there were sinuous traces of silver all over the terrace by our front door. You called me and we searched for what I suspected was a slug. We did find it, hidden in the morning dew under chestnut leaves. When you were squealing with joy at the discovery, I could not help thinking of this apparently useless, slimy animal. It was the slime that made that beautiful trace in the sun. Just like our lives, dear son, a silver trace, so short-lived, almost evanescent. That silver trace remains in my heart and I know it is inscribed in yours.

At the school of the survival of the fittest, Pat was a lion when he was young, and then he went to war. He was strong, handsome, capable, loving and kind. He came back ill and needing help; but he retained for us his silver wings and scintillating trace in the sun. His long struggle between the world of the living and that of the dead bore its fruit, in him, in me and you. I had to wear his giant's boots, and when I wore them for the first time, I felt like Tom Thumb stealing what did not belong to him. Soon, by some miracle, the boots started to fit me. I did not mind being the one who became the breadwinner.

When I came home, I had my two men waiting for me. My little king and my big king who both treated me like a queen. Your father's tenderness constantly sustained me. He was waiting for me on his couch and at night we still shared a bed and even a bit of touch-lovemaking. It was a difficult time for him when he had to recognize his impotence, following another operation and the high doses of medication. That saddened him so that he lost confidence in himself. I repeatedly told him it did not matter, and it was true. It did not matter that much. We had everything else in more quantity and quality than most couples. We loved each other to the very end.

What we kept the longest was the joy of communication. You know how I love to tell stories. I came home with bags full of anecdotes, and I talked and both of you questioned and interrupted and laughed, and I stretched out my stories, as happy as a lark giving food to its young. We shared and your father pondered and you Rex, you asked questions. In his waking hours during the night, Pat would think of the problems I was facing at work, with keeping up the house, with your education and he would propose solutions. I listened to his advice which was always sound. Happiness and unhappiness together, because of the underlying sadness, which we tried not to express.

But, you Rex, picked up on the hidden side of things as a child would, very quickly and very soon. You kept a cheerful appearance. Your father and I worried that you were growing up in too much of an adult world. We lived with lots of words but in silence also. Having you grow up with what appeared to be a man-mother and a woman-father would never have been our choice, Rex. You had to live with it every single day as your obligation and fate. One day, your childhood laughter ceased. Your liveliness was replaced by anguish. Under our roof, three anguishes were fostered and gradually festered. So entwined were the threads of our lives that none of us could unravel the skein. Who among us three would have been able to seize one single thread of the coil and run away with it?

I hoped you would be the one, dearest son, because you had youth on your side. I lost the husband; you lost the father and with him the thread. Whose fault? No one's fault, nobody's. No body. Just bodies; dead bodies. Your father's first and now, mine.

My son trembles. He salutes the arriving mourners one by one. I am silent in the coffin, but proud of him for acting like a gentleman. My heart aches at the constant shivering of his lips. White saliva lodges in the corners of his full parted lips. His large back throws a shadow on the marble, as the light shines on his light brown hair. He was so blond when he was a baby! He has cut himself shaving. His baby skin has stopped bleeding; a single tiny dry pearl of blood remains. Now he touches his cheek nervously with his too plump hand.

I am wearing my dark skirt, of fine, supple material. Fanny also chose the white blouse. 'Simple yet elegant,' she would have told me. She's got her head on her shoulders, that one, everybody agrees. She could have been my daughter. In a way, she was, and she was not. I hired her. One of the choices I never regretted. Pat had said after one of his ponderings: "Grab her quickly, now." And it was done. Fanny chose the announcement, cards, flowers, and coffin. Poor Rex just stood around, unable to function. She even chose my finest bra and panties, since the funeral director asked for them. And Rex took the doily out of the drawer.

One never talks of the need for bras and panties for a dead body. Silence on the subject. It is not censorship; it is more an embarrassment, I suppose: a cleaner version of reality, as we render death more and more sanitized, till it becomes so remote that one cannot deal with the loss. Skipping the grieving process is a mistake in my book. It's like in novels. Nobody writes about going to the bathroom. If I were still alive, I would have loved to write a book about the importance of body fluids and toilet matters in people's lives. The proof is in the pudding, as they say.

After I retired from Meriwether University, I had plenty of time to linger on the toilet and read magazines. I see people who include reading material in their toilets. Fanny and I know a famous writer who wrote his whole output on the toilet. Interesting concept of getting rid of the overflow! I like that. It is accepting a certain reality.

As for Fanny, she does have common sense and humanity, too. She was the only one at the University to keep in touch regularly after I retired. She called me and gave me news of the old place. My enemies who had accused me of fomenting all sorts of intrigues against them had soon found other targets to shoot and other cats to skin. Who would have known that after two months, I really would miss the rotten place? After Pat's death, - a death that I had wished for once or twice, in my darkest moments – words, a language did not seem to exist any longer. Retirement made me feel my isolation all the more. Rex was already turned inward by then and I had no one to speak to, to love and comfort me.

I gave all I could to dear Rex. But he lived in his shell. He desperately needed me for his stability but I needed someone to cheer me up. My affair with Harold had petered out some time before he moved to the country and was more and more absorbed in his wife's final illness, as I was also with Pat's. For both of us, our first ties came first. I was used to being busy and working. Household chores never held great interest for me. Cooking perhaps, but only if I prepared a good meal for guests. Everyday cooking was never my forte.

Thus, my inner strength was sapped. Nothingness felt heavy, and I had all that 'nothing' to carry around my neck like an albatross. The 'no more' demanded oblivion. And there were tranquilizers once in a while, when nights were too long. Once I was cleaning Rex's room when he had gone out and I found his father's gun under his bed. It petrified me. That day I almost pushed Rex out and forced him to go to a funny movie. He seemed to want to go out less and less. He had had a small automobile accident on an overpass, entering a freeway. The other driver accused him of hesitating and going too slowly; he was at fault. Since then, he has been afraid to drive on the freeway. Days seemed to become nights and nights were like days. Time was suspended. No Thursdays anymore and no Sundays either. Our world mostly black on gray. And now a gun under my son's bed. What anguish!

The shuffling of feet accelerates in the aisle. The memorial is going to begin. They all are in their pews. Seven p.m. Punctuality is *de rigueur* at such a service. Fingers fidget over the keys. Organ music rises and evokes the autumn of my life.

"The earth prepares for winter's snow." I have not had time to enjoy the leaves of this season. I have felt so poorly and so down. Night falls so early already. My mind wants to play hooky, tonight. I hear only part of the sermon. A deep voice speaks. I recognize the voice of my friend's husband:

"What seems lost in early night is found again in morning's mist."

I will not see the mist tomorrow. I suppose it is morbid to think that, irony of ironies, but I will be in the grave tomorrow! It's shocking, for it is happening to me now.

The organ exhales and stops again. My eyes go back to that young woman I do not know, sitting next to Harold. Suddenly, I experience an overwhelming feeling of happiness. What's happening? Why do I feel that this very autumn is changing into spring? A throat is cleared with a little cough. I do not recognize that person. A young woman's cough. Who is she? A young friend of Harold? A student of mine? Those Scandinavian blue eyes. That turned-up nose. Ahhh. A daughter? Too young to be a daughter. A granddaughter?

Yes, a granddaughter. Joy engulfs me.

Where does the morning light hide within the music? I wonder. Is this what came of that little voice so many years ago, in Pipestone, Minnesota? That cry? Was it in February? Of course, it was. The 8th of February to be precise. Not long before Valentine's Day. That much I remember.

Somehow Harold is sitting with my granddaughter. A miracle!

Then the voice of my friend and colleague, Fanny, breaks the silence in the chapel and brings me back to the evening harshness and its eerie ice. Their shards are softly planted in my flesh and around the wound a drop of heat trickles down to my heart.

Fanny recites a poem by Valéry:

"Ce toit tranquille où marchent les colombes
Entre les pins palpite, entre les tombes;
Midi le juste y compose de feux
La mer, la mer, toujours recommencée."

This tranquil roof where some sails
Dove-like, seem to walk,
Palpitates through pine trees, between tombs.
Impartial Noon plays with the fiery sea surface
The sea, the sea forever renewed.

The sea, good choice. I would give her an A! Once a teacher, always a teacher. One corrects, one gives a grade! I have taught this poem in my graduate class. I could be eloquent on the meaning of the symbol of the sea equated to the power of the body, that of the mind, the amniotic fluid and regeneration. Now, from the pulpit, Fanny reads a sonnet by Shakespeare:

I think good thoughts, while others write good words

From my blue silk pillow with its ecru doily, I wink at Fanny, and at that granddaughter of mine, next to Harold. And at Shakespeare, too. See, Fanny perceives my little wink and we smile at each other in between a sigh and a rhyme.

Me for my dumb thoughts, speaking in effect.

Now the last verse comes to an end. A tear appears in the corner of Fanny's eye. Other tears appear in the eyes of the blue-eyed young woman. I am thirsty. I drink their tears before they roll down their cheeks. I am finally happy. My substitute daughter, my granddaughter, thank you for being here. You love me?

I love you too.

The minister evokes the path to serenity covered with white roses leading up to Heaven. I become a young woman again, then a bride ready to join my bridegroom. I look at my hands. They have taken on a transparent quality. They look like sculpted hands of pale ochre marble. A flow of words washes over me. Humans grieve with words and with the Word. Words say, tell, create, sometimes invent or betray. If Pat had not died before me, I wonder what kind of service I would have had? He might have scattered my ashes in all the Northwest spots that we had visited.

Did I betray someone, something? Of course, I did. Who has not? Did I wish for my own death? Dear Rex, forgive me. I betray you this minute by being absent from your life. I betrayed another, too. I yearned for peace so much! My death throes lasted but five minutes and I was gone. I did not suffer long.

Thank you, Rex, for trying to revive me in my cardiac arrest. It was of no use. Don't torture yourself with questions. Did I want to die or not? No one will know but I. I started dying a long time ago. Perhaps that day in Minnesota.

I am slowly reaching the state of tranquility I have longed for. *Au revoir, mes amis.*

Good night, ladies and gentlemen, good night.

20

CONSEQUENCES
Thursday, December 10, 1987

"How can I manage? Mother died a little more than six weeks ago, and I am drowning in papers. I have received this form. I don't know what to do. How must I answer? I have to sit down and do it. Now. Listen, you stupid Rex, you must prepare a rough draft and deal with it." Rex rubs the snot off his nose with the back of his hand and sits down, heavily.

Disheveled, unwashed, in smelly clothes, he remains seated at his mother's desk in their house, HIS house now, in the woods. He puts his head on the desk. He does not move.

He wakes up from his trance and starts to write:

I recognize the terms of the transfer from North-Western....

But not from Commonwealth, Boston.

The form 9810 should be coming and the request for prompt assessment....

Intend to withdraw funds from Corporation...

I will call you when I receive the form from Commonwealth from Boston...

Monday, December 19, 1988 at 7:15 p.m.

Rex shuffles towards the telephone in his worn-out slippers. He picks up the receiver.

"Hello, Boyd's Supermarket? This is Rex Murray. I would like you to deliver one case of Elk Cove Wine, pinot noir, to 851 Fir Grove Road, please."

A long silence.

"Yes, you have my credit card on file. OK. Thanks. Bye."

At 7:25 p.m. Rex picks up the telephone again to make another phone call.

"Hi, Grimaldi's Pizza? Can I order a large pizza pepperoni with black olives and mushrooms?"

"How long?"

"Yes, it's Rex. You recognized my voice?"

"Yes, that's it, on Fir Grove Road. See you in half an hour. Thank you very much."

Tuesday, December 20, 1988

"What am I doing? I'm 37. I have no one. It's just before Christmas. Mooooootheerrr, Faatheeerrr! Where am I?"

"Where is my paper? Where are my ballpoints all in different colors? My pencil?"

Friday, December 23, 1988

Words on a scrap of paper

Appetite

   Sleep

         Shift mood dramatic

Hallucinations

             sexual excitement
_____

   colors of outside

                  Screen red

xarax

3pm Monday

225-   655 0943   -------*apprehension*

- *hear*

- *threat*

-

- *Winter..*
Summer

- *dry*

- *Humid*

When next

Trying

Humidity humidifier   heater
Dryness temperature
dust

Acoustics -   boards -   floor
Crazy name

Alert when I wake up
Pepped **up**   ▯masturbation
frequent thirst & urination

more normal in late afternoon
evening at 5... *feel   very very......*
sore throat at times

several more sore sore .... lemon

2   **PIANO**

feel
very sexy

not hungry   in morning   mourning

11:30   22ⁿᵈ and NORTHRUP

2pm   play… piano_____

Rex Patrick Murray was found dead at his home the day after Christmas, Monday 26, 1988, at 5 p.m.

Fanny Taylor had called the police that Monday at 4:30 p.m., when she was unable to reach Rex. One week earlier, Rex had refused to come and share their Christmas dinner on Sunday 25, 1988.

21

END MATTERS
Papers of Rex Murray's estate, 1991

PORTLAND CENTER FOR INTERNAL MEDICINE
Internal Medicine and Urology

2322 NW Locust
Portland, Or 97219 (503) 224-5261
R. Robert Bouvakian, M.D.
K. L. Kohl, M.D.

March 10, 1989

John R. Watanabe
Attorney at Law,
513 Pike St., Suite 640
Seattle, WA 98140

Dear Mr. Watanabe:

I understand from your letter of March 3, 1989 that there are some problems with the Internal Revenue Service with regard to the estate of the Murray family: Patrick Emmet Murray, Judith Carol Jensen Murray, and Rex Patrick Murray, all now deceased. The three Murrays were patients of mine at various times and I would like to make a few comments from a medical standpoint in hopes that they might help clarify the situation with the Internal Revenue Service.

I believe the problems with IRS began with Mr. Patrick E. Murray, who died in January of 1981. Mr. Murray had many medical reasons for not being totally competent to handle the responsibility of filing complete or accurate tax returns during the last two or three years of his life. As you know, Mr. Murray had suffered for many years from acute and chronic renal failure and succumbed in January, 1981 to terminal heart failure. Mr. Murray had suffered from chronic respiratory insufficiency of a severe degree and his judgment was impaired and his intellectual functioning compromised on this basis. In addition, he had had a stroke in 1980. I talked to him on many occasions and he appeared quite depressed over the fact that his health had reduced him to a dependent capacity. He felt somehow ashamed and had a sense of worthlessness at being unable to function as the breadwinner of the family. He clung to his perceived responsibility as tax-filer for the family as one way of relieving the burden on his wife and of making himself useful to the family unit even past the time when he was actually able to fulfill this task appropriately.

Mrs. Murray, who died in October, 1986 of a myocardial infarction, suffered also from chronic depression, which became acute in the five years following her husband's death. She used sleeping-aids and tranquilizers which could have contributed to serious impairment of judgment in her business and professional dealings, certainly including her dealings with the Internal Revenue Service. Further information on Mrs. Murray's psychological state could probably be obtained from Dr. Roger Weinstein, a Portland psychiatrist whom I know she consulted from time to time.

Dr. Weinstein could also provide helpful information concerning Rex P. Murray, whom I saw very little. I know he was a patient of Dr. Weinstein over a period of many years. One of the real burdens for Patrick Murray was his concern about the future of his son, Rex, who had had his first severe psychological break in the summer after his graduation from an eastern prep school. I know that the Murrays had hoped and expected that Rex would continue his education at the University of California, Berkeley, but he was never able to do so after his breakdown in 1970. Rex's physical health was not compromised, and I only saw him once or twice for rather minor problems, but his psychological health was never strong and Dr. Weinstein could provide more pertinent information to that effect. I believe you have the information that the official cause of his death in December, 1988 was alcoholic poisoning and that in itself certainly suggests an impairment which would have rendered appropriate business dealings, including tax filings, difficult or impossible for Rex Murray.

As I think back over the years of my acquaintance with the Murray family and realize that they were trying to handle their own business affairs, such as income tax returns, I feel quite ashamed that I did not recognize this and advise them otherwise.

Somehow it is always a difficult point in the physician-patient relationship to decide when it is appropriate or perhaps even necessary to assert one's opinions in non-medical matters in the patient's life. I certainly feel obligated to write this letter on behalf of these former patients of mine, because I believe that, medically speaking, there was absolutely no way that they could have been considered competent to carry out their obligations toward the IRS the last few years of their lives. I would hope that if you or the Internal Revenue Service wish to discuss this issue with me further, you would not hesitate to contact me. The Murray family were a special trio, valiant in so many ways, tragic in so many others. In honor of their memory, I would want to be of any possible help.

Sincerely,
R. Robert Bouvakian, M.D   RRB: jer

Daniel J. Barker
2441 Thunder Mt. Drive,
San Bernardino, CA

January 22, 1991

John R. Watanabe
Attorney at Law,
513 Pike St., Suite 640
Seattle, WA, 98140

Dear Mr. Watanabe:

In a recent conversation with an old friend of my mother, I learned that my cousin Rex Patrick Murray died about two years ago. My mother, Vera Murray Barker, who died in 1983, was the sister of Rex Murray's father, Patrick E. Murray. I found your address among my mother's papers on a letter you had written her in 1981, after my Uncle Pat's death, concerning the family home in Sherman, Illinois which my uncle and my mother had owned together. You also wrote to inform my mother of Carol Murray's death in 1986 but my mother had died three years earlier.

I believe that my sister Susan and I may have been Rex's only living relatives. I was wondering how the Murray estate was disposed of. I realize this might be confidential, but as the only living relatives, it seems to me that my sister and I should be entitled to know what was included in Rex's will.

I would appreciate hearing from you.

Very truly yours,

Daniel J. Barker

Watanabe, Fillmore, and Jones, Attorneys at Law
513 Pike St., Suite 640
Seattle, OR, 98104

January 29, 1991

Mr. Daniel J. Barker
2441 Thunder Mt. Drive,
San Bernardino, CA

Dear Mr. Barker:

I received your letter asking for information concerning the last will and testament of your cousin, Rex Patrick Murray. Since there was nothing particularly sensitive about Mr. Murray's will, and since, as you say, you and your sister appear to be the only living relatives, I am able to share some basic information with you without violating any trust. This account will not include dollar amounts nor specific beneficiaries, in order to protect client privacy, but I can give you the following information:

1. Your cousin Rex and his mother, J. Carol Jensen Murray, had me draw up their wills within months after Rex's father's death, ten years ago. No changes were ever made in the wills in later years.
2. The wills were simple. Each party left everything to the other and then, on the death of the last survivor, which was Rex, of course, everything was to be left, share and share alike, to two well-known and well-respected national charities which specialize in helping the underprivileged.

3. The personal representative named for the estate was Ms. Julie Bellfield, a former student of Professor Murray and a close personal friend of the family.
4. The disposition of the estate required four steps, organized by Ms. Bellfield and myself:
    a. Conversion of investments (stocks and bonds) to cash.
    b. Preparation of personal belongings for sale.
    c. Sale of personal belongings at auction.
    d. Sale of house and car.

The house was sold in late spring of 1989 and, in fact, has since been demolished and three new houses built on the property.

No personal bequests whatsoever were made in the will. Both Professor Murray and Rex Murray were understandably distraught after Patrick Murray's death and insisted that it was important to keep their wills very simple and straightforward.

I hope this information is helpful to you and your sister. I thought very highly of all the Murrays and was proud to believe that they considered me a friend as well as their lawyer. If I can be of any further assistance to you, please let me know.

Very truly,
John R. Watanabe

22

THE GRAND-DAUGHTER'S RETURN
Summer 2003

"What's that address again, Peter?" Caroline asked, steering the Explorer carefully along the winding road.

"0851 SW Fir Grove Road," replied Peter, her eight-year-old son. Caroline and Peter remained quiet in the car as a thoughtful Dave Matthews ballad played on the car radio.

"O.K. There, I see 0314, so it should be a little farther along on the left."

"This area looks very familiar. I think I drove along here back in 1986."

"Did you come to Portland then? That was even before I was born." Peter inquired.

"Oh, yes. I was still going to school and Dad and I weren't even engaged yet. I came for a funeral, the funeral of an old friend of Grandma, named Carol Murray. Before the service, I remember driving by the house where Mrs. Murray used to live. It seems to me it was in this general area. I know it was near that college, those buildings over there on the left. Now watch the numbers. I think the house we're looking for will be around the next curve."

As they rounded the bend in the road, three large houses, built in the early 1990's, loomed side by side on the left.

"There, it's the second one, with the big fir trees behind it. That must be the realtor's car. She said she'd meet us here."

An hour later, as Caroline and Peter were driving back to their rented home, they discussed the house.

"Did you like that house, Peter?'

"Yeah, I like it a lot. And I like all the trees. It feels like you're in the woods."

"I like it, too. I think it might work well for our family. It looks big from the outside, but if we use those two extra rooms on the first floor for Dad's and my offices, that only leaves two extra bedrooms. We need those for when Aunt Margie or Aunt Annie and the kids come for a visit."

"Can they come soon?"

"I hope so. If Dad likes the house, I think we could be in it by the beginning of August, so we'd have time for a visit before school starts."

"I'm so glad we live closer to Jay and Stevie now. When we lived in San Francisco, we hardly ever saw them."

"Yes, it's definitely easier to get together now. Living in Portland would be better than San Francisco. And you like getting together with your cousins, don't you?" Caroline smiled fondly at her son's cheerful, freckled face.

"Well, sure. When we lived in California, other kids talked all the time about their families and I felt like I didn't have any family, but now I do."

Caroline thought with satisfaction that the move north had been a good one for all of them. Peter, solid, steady little person that he was, had often seemed lonely in California and he relished the increased contact with Jim's large, warmhearted family who lived scattered around the Portland area. Jim enjoyed his new job here, developing microchip technology and the company was strong and growing. Caroline herself should be able to find a good executive position in the Portland area. She had talked to a few people last week and one of the bank officials was encouraging; there were hints that a middle management position could be available in early Fall. The Senior Vice-President had suggested she come talk to him in August.

"Are we going to bring Dad to see the house in the trees?" asked Peter.

"Oh, I think we should, don't you? Let's bring him tonight after dinner. The realtor gave me a key and it stays light till after nine, so we'll have plenty of time to show Dad around."

That evening, the three of them explored the big, modern house, bigger that they would have chosen first, but well-organized and conveniently located.

"Will the commute from here be good, Jim?"

"Oh, yes. It'll actually be shorter than my drive now from our rental. I should be able to make it in half an hour. That's only half what I drove in California, so by comparison it seems like a piece of cake."

"Of course, it would be really easy if we bought one of those country homes out around your company's plant."

"Yes, but remember, they all are identical. I don't like that. And we talked about wanting to be closer to the city. This is a good compromise, I think. A manageable commute, a nice forest feel, and an easy drive to downtown."

"There's just something about this area that feels like home to me. It's so peaceful. And I love all that woodsy area across the street. The realtor said it was a Convent until recently, but now it belongs to that small college we passed on the way here."

Caroline realized she hadn't seen their son for several minutes. "Where's Peter?"

"I think he ran outside again. He loves that little thicket at the back of the property. I'll lock up here if you want to go find him."

Caroline emerged into the soft, late June twilight and walked around to the back of the house. She called, "Peter. Peter."

"I'm here, Mom. Look at these neat trees."

"Oh, yes. That's bamboo. That's quite a bunch!"

"Some of the trees have fallen down and look, I can even lift them. Maybe Dad and I can build a little house back here. Stevie and Jay and I could have a clubhouse. That would be so neat!"

"That's a great idea," Caroline said. She stood still in the tender evening light, listening to the sigh of the breeze in the tops of the fir trees and the answering rustle of the bamboo leaves.

This could be our home. This could be the place that Peter remembered his childhood in. And, smiling, she walked with her son back to where her husband was waiting.

The next day, they signed the papers to get their new house in Portland.

23

CAROLINE

In Caroline's head a new rhythm was born. The repeated sounds of crashing waves on the jagged reefs of life were Carol's life, waves imprinting themselves in Caroline's brain.

The Pacific Ocean, always part of her personal music, was now marking her with an indelible tattoo. And it would be her son's inheritance. The rippling waters of the San Francisco Bay resonated with her childhood as well as with the time she spent as a young woman studying at Berkeley. The flowing rivers of western Oregon where Jim's family lived had attracted them legato to the Northwest and on up to the shining shores of Puget Sound. The sea pines, the rustling reeds of the wetland wilds formed an Oriental garden that spread throughout the Pacific Northwest. These Oregon landscapes and their songs would be their new life and their legacy to Peter.

A new trio was created in the Northwest: a hopeful young woman with her husband and their son.

Caroline knew that she had found a real home for her family, at the same place where Carol and her family lived.

Deep inside, she recognized that her own voyage would be happier and smoother than Carol's.

The coincidence of her name still amazed her. She had a longer version of Carol's name. She would continue the genetic line of their connected identities, even if she had but a vague idea of her biological grandmother's life.

The "-line" of her own first name in Caro-line would extend the written line of Carol's story.

Call it a new life in the memory of Carole with an "e."

Acknowledgments

I thank Sheila Cullen for her friendship and advice.

25000711R00141

Made in the USA
San Bernardino, CA
08 February 2019